Also by Péter Nádas

A Book of Memories

The End of a
Family Story

The End of a Family Story

A Novel by

Péter Nádas

Translated from the Hungarian by

Imre Goldstein

Farrar, Straus and Giroux

New York

Farrar, Straus and Giroux
19 Union Square West, New York 10003

Copyright © 1977 by Péter Nádas
Translation copyright © 1998 by Farrar, Straus and Giroux, Inc.
All rights reserved
Distributed in Canada by Douglas & McIntyre Ltd.
Printed in the United States of America
First published in 1977 by Szépirodalmi Könyvkiadó, Budapest,
Hungary, as *Egy családregény vége*
Designed by Jonathan D. Lippincott
First American edition, 1998

Library of Congress Cataloging-in-Publication Data
Nádas, Péter, 1942–
    [Családregény története. English]
    The end of a family story : a novel / by Péter Nádas ;
    translated from the Hungarian by Imre Goldstein.
        p. cm.
    ISBN 0-374-14832-5 (alk. paper)
    I. Goldshtain, Imri, 1938– . II. Title.
PH3291.N297C7313 1998
894'.511334—dc21   98-7887

And the light shineth in the darkness; and the darkness comprehended it not.

—John 1:5

The End of a
Family Story

nursery. We had lined this room with hay to make it nice and soft. I sat down at the edge of the bed and drew the child's head onto my lap. I could dig my fingers into his wet hair; I hugged him. As if my own mother were hugging me. I could flatten my palm against his clammy forehead and wouldn't know whether it was my own palm I felt or his forehead. A thick vein was bulging out on his neck. If I cut that vein, all his blood would flow out. In the kitchen Mama was always making a racket with the pots. "Hurry up with that story, Papa, we'll be late for the party!" She was always in a hurry to go to some party, but I did not rush with the story because it felt good sitting there like that, with the child's wet head on my lap. "What story should I tell you?" The child opened his eyes. "I'd like to hear about the tree again." The way he looked at me made me think not of the story but of how good it would be if he really were my child, lying like this on my lap. "Very well, then, I'll tell you about the tree; close your eyes and listen. Once upon a time there was a tree. This special tree had a leaf. Of course it had thousands of leaves, but the one I'm telling you about was a very special leaf, not like the others. The tree in my story stood in a haunted garden. Nobody really knew this garden, people only knew that somewhere there was such a garden. But search as they might, they couldn't find it. And there were plenty of searchers, too. They even used those sniffing police dogs. Stop fidgeting! From the street the garden couldn't be seen. Not even from an airplane. But we knew how to get in. Behind a bush was the entrance to the secret tunnel. Through the tunnel, from the street, straight into the garden! Bats lived in this secret tunnel. They were there to protect the garden. Bats have stinking bodies. But we went anyway, because I knew all I had to do was yell, Fly away, bats, don't come back or I'll stick you in my sack! That made the bats hide in the darkest corners of the tunnel. Because we also took along a flashlight, a good strong one. But the passage was still not clear, because that's when the octopuses came. They had eyes like spotlights, made of reflectors. If someone strayed into the tunnel, right away they started swimming toward him. These are amphibious octopuses that can swim very fast in the air, too. At night they come out of their caves, but then they don't use their eyes, because they don't want to be seen. Anyway, if somebody wanders in there, zoom! they get him, they wrap themselves around him, hug him tight, and twist him until they've squeezed the last bit of life out of him. As we were walking we noticed that the floor of the cave was strewn with bones. Because lots of people wandered into the cave, but none of them ever reached the garden. This we hadn't figured in our plans. We thought that once we got past the bats the passage would be clear." Grandmama lay in bed all day sucking on sourballs. They

stories. "Now I will tell you about the happy times of my life." And then he would tell me about all those happy times. Or he would say, "Now I will tell you how I escaped from the jaws of death. Once, on the third of January, 1915, we went on a patrol with my hussars. There was a great fog all over Serbia that day. As we were riding, I heard some strange hoofbeats. I thought to myself it was our own horses with the thick fog doubling the sound of their hooves. Then in a few seconds strange riders emerged from the fog. They were like shadows, but there was no time to think. We were so close to them that if horses weren't smarter than people we would have collided. The horses were rearing up and neighing. And that damn Serb had already drawn his sword! So I drew mine! We clashed. But he had the advantage because he was above me, standing on higher ground. I stab, he slashes—and if I hadn't crouched, making myself small in the saddle, my head would have flown right off. As it was, he only got my hat. Well, I said to myself, it's all over for me. But then one of my hussars was suddenly on the spot. By the time that damn Serb could raise his sword again to bring it down from above—he could have sliced me and my horse right in half!—my hussar had chopped off his head." Grandpapa laughed so hard when he told me this story, his denture fell out, loose in his mouth. Always he'd manage to shove it neatly back in place. "That was my first great escape. Or maybe

me a story about my mother. But she waited until I fell asleep. I preferred made-up stories. When I played the Papa and we put the child to bed, I always made up a story. The story about the tree continued with our getting hold of two sticks. "And those octopuses came at us! A hundred of 'em! Each octopus had fifty tentacles. I was whacking away! They saw they couldn't do anything to us! And in a jiffy, we were in the garden! All they could do was look at our backs! But then we had an eyeful, too! Because this garden was full of trees. Very special trees! Trees of every kind, but we couldn't tell just what kind. The one we thought was a peach tree had plums hanging from it, along with cherries, sour cherries, and even bunches of grapes. We could eat to our heart's content. But the tree I want to tell you about we only noticed later." But I didn't go on with the story. A strange head was asleep on my lap. I didn't know myself how I'd gotten here. Through a half-open mouth it was breathing evenly. Somewhere, far away, a car stopped, but the engine kept idling. It was as if I saw myself sleeping in my own lap. It would have felt so good to lower my head next to his, to sleep alongside him. Carefully I lifted my hand from his forehead. He felt it, stirred a little, and closed his mouth. Now he was breathing noisily through his nose. The engine of the car was purring out on the street. I'd have liked to have a fore-head like his, but on mine the hair grew from lower

down, and I was ashamed of that. Éva was still scrub-
bing the pots in the kitchen. The heat seemed stuck,
there was no breeze to move it. Though the spots of
light were quivering, their rhythm was unpredictable.
One tiny spot was moving on his forehead, lit a trail
into his hair, then vanished. I was sorry I'd taken my
hand away. I would have liked to feel again that my
hand was his forehead. "Why aren't you telling him
the story?" "He's asleep. Not pretending, he's really
fallen asleep." Éva put the pot on the shelf. The shelf
is a piece of wood between two branches, but we call
it the kitchen cabinet. If we kicked the branches, the
pots, full of holes, fell to the ground. Then Éva would
always say, "Papa, the kitchen cabinet fell apart, it's
really time you fixed it!" But this time the pots didn't
fall down, though when she slipped in next to me and
tried to be careful, she did kick the bush. I could smell
her. It seemed as if not the light but her skin was quivering. "We have to get to the party!" She was wearing
tiny bathing shorts and a bra with frills. No matter
how much she pulled and tugged at her breasts, they
hadn't grown large enough to fill the bra. For the party
we would always crawl out from under the bushes,
her pink tulle outfit reaching to the ground, and she'd
say she was also wearing jewelry. "One mustn't wear
too much. A woman should wear only a few pieces,
but they should be expensive and chosen carefully, you
understand?" Everyone would be watching her. When

Grandpapa. I thought that if he hadn't turned out like Grandpapa, then I wouldn't turn out like him. I was usually still asleep when he had to go, but he'd come over and kiss me and draw his finger across my mouth. His face then would be smooth, only his clothes would smell of benzene. Whenever Grandpapa started to talk he would always yell. When he wasn't talking, he would clasp his hands, slip them between his knees, let his head droop, his shoulders would sag, and it was hard to see how big he was. And if he couldn't talk to anybody for a long time, he'd fall asleep in the armchair. Father crossed his legs when he sat; with one elbow he'd lean on his knee, hold his cigarette in his other hand, then suddenly he'd jump up and begin pacing around the room. He kept lifting things and looking at them as if seeing them for the first time. He would smell the food. And he'd also draw his fingers across the furniture. And when he had had enough of walking about, he'd lie down on the bed; I could tell he would have liked to sleep, he even closed his eyes, but then he'd look up and for no reason at all burst out laughing. "Why are you laughing?" He'd wrinkle his forehead. "I'm laughing? No, I'm not. It's nothing. Maybe I thought of something amusing." Sometimes I'd try to see what happened when I laughed. So I'd laugh, but he wouldn't ask me why. If he had, I would have told him that I laughed to see how he felt when he laughed. In the evening I was allowed to lie next to him in his bed and I'd ask him to tell me a story. "A story? Let's see now! I swear I can't think of a single story, nothing. Wait! Should I tell you about the boots? All right. Once upon a time, way beyond the seven seas, there were two boots. They were a real pair. And they were friends. Such good friends that nobody could imagine one without the other. Whenever one took a step, so did the other. When the other stopped, the one did, too. That's why one boot was called One and the other was called Other. And One and Other were together not only during the day but at night, too. Every night they stood at the foot of the bed. They liked to sleep like that, standing up. They didn't get very tired, because they leaned on each other. They both liked to feel the skin of the other. Actually they had no other wish than to stay like that. That's how they lived their lives. But slowly they grew old. They were thrown out, on the garbage heap. One was thrown to the right, the other to the left. And then—and then I don't know what happened. That's the end of the story. Go to sleep now." But I didn't want to believe that was the end of it. However, I had to go back to my own bed. "And the boots, whatever happened to the boots?" I asked him when he came home again and I was lying next to him in the dark. "What boots?" "The boots that were friends." "Oh, the boots! I don't know, I've no idea what happened to them." When he left on the morning train I thought

us eating ourselves silly with all that fruit, then lying down on the grass. "Our stomachs were so full we couldn't even close our eyes. As we are lying there we notice a tree branch bending over us; the tree was like all the other trees and the branch was like all the other branches. Still, at the tip of this branch was one leaf that was very special. It would stir as if it were nodding. As if it were saying something we couldn't understand. None of the other leaves moved, just this one. Then it too stopped moving. We got scared, 'cause this must have meant something, and what would happen if we didn't understand what the leaf said? Then it moved again. But not like before; not like this but like that, as if this time it didn't want something to happen, I mean it wasn't nodding like before. The other leaves didn't move at all. Leaves have a special language, but you can learn it only with a magic drink. Then the leaf spoke to us for the third time. It started out slowly, got faster, then slowed down, got very slow, to be sure we understood it. But we didn't. We'd better get out of here and look for that magic drink. If we had understood the leaf we could have stayed in the garden until the day we died." He opened his eyes. I thought we'd start fighting. "There is no such garden, and leaves can't talk!" "Yes, they can!" If he started the fight, I wouldn't try to stop him. He could beat me as much as he wanted to. Even if I started the fight he would win. But I still didn't

place. As a witness!" She put on her white hat and looked at herself in the mirror. It was no use asking her to take me with her. She said it was something very serious and she had a very important job to do. A secret one. I already knew that my head could pass through between the iron bars. It didn't matter that she locked the door. On the terrace where their mother in her dressing gown used to yell, two men were standing. Smoking cigarettes. The tub was floating in the pool. Our game was to pull the plug, let the ship sink, and then the pirates won. I saw Grandmama's hat bobbing past the stair banister. One of the men led Grandmama into the house, the other kept smoking and looking at the garden. It was all right; he couldn't have known I was there, watching him. Sometimes I thought about how there were people who didn't know I existed at all. It was getting dark. For a long time nobody came out. I tried to imagine the house search. The attic. The cellar. Sometimes, when Grandmama left the house, I'd rummage around in the closets. I was afraid that in the cellar they'd discover our other apartment, the one we built in the winter. One of the men came out, carrying suitcases that scraped along the gravel path. They'll probably move away from here. And now the other man was there, too. Together they went back into the house. Or maybe their father had come back from Argentina. The men carried a table out to the terrace. Grandmama still hadn't come out. They went back in again. The two of them carried out an armchair. The other chairs they just threw out, one after the other, sliding the chairs along the smooth stone. One of them got stuck on something and tipped over. There were some loud words, then everything went quiet again. All I could think of was that either they were moving away or going on vacation. And yet I knew that's not what it was. The night before I dreamed that Grandpapa was standing in the middle of the room because he had to leave. Still, I believed that if I hugged him, if I cried, if I begged him not to go, he would stay. But as I pressed my face to his I felt how stubbly it was, because he used to shave only every other day. When Grandmama came home she said she was very tired. She'd tired herself out. She put her white hat and white pocketbook on the table. "We found ten kilograms of sugar, two large containers of fat, and thirty pairs of nylon stockings. Thirty. And all that jewelry!" She shut the window so the bugs wouldn't come in and buzz around the light. She promised that if I went to bed with no trouble she'd tell me the legend of Genaéva.

a different black dress, the gray one. The gold butterfly she kept in a steel box and she always carried the key with her. From the window of my room I could see the garden gate. The windows were very high, the sills very wide, because the house was very old. If Grandmama left the house I'd run to the window to peek after her, to see her disappear among the trees in the street. Sometimes she'd come back because she forgot something. She was afraid something might catch on fire, and while she was standing in line at the market I'd go up in flames. I thought about that, what that would be like. My head could just get through between the two middle uprights of the iron bars. I would open the window and slip out. Or, if the house caught on fire in the summer, the window would be open anyway. Gábor said his father told him that if someone's head can get through an opening there is nothing to be afraid of, because that means his whole body can get through. But Gábor probably made that up, because his father is in Argentina, which is where he sends those packages from. They got chocolate and figs, too, in the packages. I had to stand by the window for a long time. Grandmama sometimes would be halfway to the store and then turn back to check the pilot light in the bathroom. The pilot light might set the house on fire. We did have a couple of boxes of matches in their cellar, but it was Gábor and Éva who got them. When Grandmama left she locked the

somebody could hide behind it. That's why I had to look behind the doors, too. Grandmama said that her grandmother had told her stories about the white wall serpent. This serpent lives in the wall. At night, in the great silence, it can be heard crawling inside the wall, eating away at it. If it crawls out of the wall, it means somebody is going to die in that room. Every house has its wall serpent. It's not green or brown, and it's not speckled, but completely white, like the wall. It never moved during the day, only the floor creaked if I walked on it. In the hallway a huge mirror hung over the telephone, and in this mirror I could see myself talking to myself on the telephone. A dark room opened from the hallway; it was full of closets and had no windows. And it, too, had a large mirror hanging on the wall. I could look at myself in it when I put on different clothes. The green velvet dress I wanted to give to Éva so she could wear it when we went to the party. Around the waist of this dress, inside a small pouch sewn into the lining, I felt some hard little thingamajigs. When I cut open the pouch with scissors, small gray disks fell out. I showed them to Gábor and Éva and told them that these were gold pieces left for us by our ancestors, who had painted them gray so other people wouldn't know what they were. Gábor took one and tapped it against his teeth. He said they weren't made of gold but of lead and they could be melted down. Before melting them down he asked me to come with him somewhere, but told Éva to stay because where we were going was none of her business. Éva didn't want to stay in the room. Gábor and I went into a room I'd never been in before. Éva ran out into the garden, crying, because Gábor beat her up. A piano stood in the middle of this room, its lid propped up with a rod. I went to the piano and looked inside because I thought that was the reason we'd come to this room. Grandmama told me that once she had a child who died because somebody was careless in propping up the lid of the grain bin and the lid fell on the child's head. I really liked the inside of the piano, because all the wires were nice and straight. But it wasn't the piano he wanted to show me, only a bottle he took out of the closet, full of some white stuff. He wanted me to smell it. It was pretty stinky. "You don't know what this is, do you?" He was shaking it in front of my nose. "That's where they squirt the cream so Mother won't get pregnant!" At the bottom of the closet I found a large paper box. We could rummage around in it for a long time because they kept lots of things in it. Shawls made of silk. A velvet handbag studded with beads and with nice soft leather inside. Two fans. Brown photographs. Letters in pink-lined envelopes. In the photographs, people I didn't know. A woman sitting on a camel and behind her you could see two pyramids. In another picture this same woman leaning against a railing and looking at the water, seeming very sad. There was a picture in which she was in a big hat and laughing. This big hat, folded up, was also there in the box, but in the picture the hat was prettier and the woman's belly was large. I found a brassiere stuffed with foam-rubber breasts. I kept squeezing them. I could tear out little pieces of rubber, but they weren't good as erasers. I also found some kind of instrument in the box; hard, black, long; at one end it had a hole; at the other end of this long black part was a red rubber ball. I could take this ball off the black thing. If I filled it with water, screwed it back on the black thing, and then squeezed it, the water squirted out through the hole. Sometimes I'd stand up on a chair and pee into the sink. In the bathroom I found a secret door. In the closet, behind the robes, was a big white button. At first I didn't know what it was for. But I kept pushing and turning it until I found out. I'd go into the closet and pull the door shut behind me. It would get dark and warm. In that strange smell of dressing gowns, I'd feel out where the button was. If I yanked it hard enough a little door would open in the rear wall of the closet and I could crawl out under the stairs. I knew that if ever I was chased by somebody I could escape through this secret door. One time I opened this door, but I didn't get to the place under the stairs. Everybody was already gone. On the wall they left a long mirror in a gilt frame. Dark curtains covered the windows. But you couldn't see out. Once when the people were still here, some-body said that the curtains were not to be drawn open. But the door was ajar and I could walk into the other room. I started walking and I could see myself in the mirror, walking. I was looking at myself because I didn't think it was me but somebody who looked like me, walking in my place. But it *was* me. I recognized the shoes on my feet, gold shoes with high heels which I'd forgotten to put back in their box. And I could see the line of rooms, one empty room after the other, and everywhere the dark curtains. The candles in the chan-deliers were not lit but it wasn't dark. Light was com-ing from someplace. I wasn't frightened, Grandmama couldn't see me here, but it wasn't very good, because I could only go forward, and from every room another one opened, just like the one before, and from there another, and I didn't know how long I'd have to keep going before I'd get there. I'd been sent somewhere. Maybe if I could peek out into the garden I could fig-ure it out! The curtains were moving a little. Behind them there were no windows! Why? But I did remem-ber where the different pieces of furniture used to stand; after all, I used to live here, and now I'd simply been sent back here. In the meantime, everything had changed. All dusty. Needed a good cleaning. I didn't see a broom anywhere. Then it occurred to me that in the last room everything had stayed the way it used to be, in the very last room, and I started to run through

really fast. The captain was afraid to come on deck because of the whales, he was only looking out through a little porthole. The pirate ship is coming! Pirates! What should he do? Black flag on the pirate ship. I kept signaling with a white handkerchief. The sky was beginning to darken. By the time the pirate ship was really close, it was thundering. And lightning. Frogs were falling from the sky. The captain had never seen anything like it before. Waves shot across the deck and whales were flying on top of the waves. I gave the last signal. The captain ran out on deck and wanted to shoot me, but in that instant a huge wave came, and splash! I threw him into the sea. Then the pirates steered alongside us and jumped over. They hugged me and kissed me. We robbed the big ship. Took everything we wanted." With a knife I scraped the valuable labels off the suitcases. The ones with the palm trees and the blue sea I gave to Csider, because he gave me cartridges in exchange. Cartridges he stole from his father. The stairs led to the upper floor. That's where they lived while Grandpapa could still walk. Grandpapa would come down the stairs slowly, holding on to the railing. But he didn't want to live downstairs because his armchair was upstairs in front of the window, and from there he had such a nice view of the garden. After lunch Grandpapa would fall asleep in his armchair. When he couldn't walk any-more, they put his armchair in front of the window in

tient people are unhappy because they always want something and always get what they don't want. That's why happiness is like the most beautiful woman. It's a mystery. It takes brains, brains! If you pretend not to notice her, if you pretend not to give her a thought, she'll throw herself at you, panting. Finesse, that's what you need to manage in life, finesse. Cunning. You've got to know how to outfox, cheat, and fool even yourself, if you have to. That's how I've done it! Acting as if I didn't wish for anything or want anything! Letting the years go by while I sit around, huddle and crouch, biding my time, waiting for the right moment. Yes, that's how I've done it! And what's happened? What have I gained? I've always been laughed at. Well, let them laugh. The unhappy ones! The idiots! They just don't know! They don't know that one must not seek happiness outside, only inside. You understand? Inside. In yourself! You must feel happiness in yourself, and when you do, never let it go! You mustn't! Not for an instant! If you let it go for the wink of an eye, that miserable happiness of yours will fly off and its place will fill with spit and snot. And then you'll be full of desires, waiting impatiently for other pleasures you may get, and there's no end to it, because all your pleasures will fill you with the lack of some other pleasure. Then something will always be missing. Missing! Missing! Then you'll want more and more, you'll want to gobble and to

Mustn't give in! They were forbidden, and I didn't let them fool my desires. Still, at night, in bed, I was lost no matter how hard I tried to hold out whenever a naked woman crossed my dreams. Yet I never touched a woman and I never tapped my own body for pleasure, either, because I was preserving myself for the moment I knew would have to come. I waited! How reluctant Noah was to lose his virginity, no matter how much they egged him on. He waited. He waited until God found Naamah for him, Enoch's daughter, the only woman since Istehar who'd remained pure in that depraved generation. I waited!" If Grandmama came into the room she would make some noise by pushing the chairs around so that Grandpapa would notice, and if he didn't, then Grandmama would also start shouting. "Again? You're doing it again? Papa, don't you realize you're talking out loud?" "Out loud? What do you mean loud?" Grandpapa would yell. "In front of the child! Telling him things like that!" But the louder she wanted to shout the softer her voice became and the louder Grandpapa's. "In front of the child? The child already knows everything! Life is already in the child, just as a single drop has all the ocean in it!" "Oh, shut up, you and your ocean!"— Grandmama was whispering, even though she wanted to yell, but she started to cough—"Ocean!" Whenever Grandpapa was not allowed to talk, he would press both his hands between his knees and fall asleep. His

teeth on the windowsill or on the table. I liked to sit nearby and watch him sleep. His mouth would open, he'd breathe loudly, as if the whole room were breathing along with him. I noticed that if I sat opposite him and listened to his breathing long enough, my own breath would also go in and out slowly and exactly at the same time as Grandpapa's. Try as I might to do it differently, his breathing seemed to be controlling mine. Then I'd grow sleepy. I also noticed that if I kept watching him for a very long time without falling asleep, he'd close his mouth, smack his lips, and look at me. I liked it when he looked at me. One afternoon, while I was lying on the bed, it was very dark but I didn't know whether I was awake or asleep, I kept feeling around to find out where I was. But touching things around me didn't help, it was so dark I had no idea where I was. I was groping about for a long time and still I couldn't see anything, only blackness, the kind of blackness in which you can't see anything, and I had no clue how I'd gotten to where I was, or where I was, or whether I was asleep, because everything around me was very hot, and it seemed to me as if in this blackness some other blackness was groping, trying to catch me, and I knew I was reaching out, too, and I thought my hands felt something but I couldn't tell exactly what, and somebody, I don't know why, kept screaming, a terrible scream, but I didn't know who, because I didn't know where I was,

even store-bought fat was better than oil because fat was nourishing. The house she was born in stood opposite the church. They'd slaughter as many as four hogs in one winter and always had plenty of lard. With Grandmama we went to visit relatives. They put lots of meat and sausages on the table. The sun was shining in the courtyard, and they said I shouldn't do anything while they went to church. I kept throwing pebbles into the well, and still they weren't back. By the time they returned I was in the pantry eating sausages. I had to climb on top of a sack to reach them. They killed a chicken, but it ran away, its head dangling to the side. I put the sausage on a plate, next to it I put bread and a big knife. First I cut a little piece of sausage and quickly ate it. Then I cut a thicker slice and didn't eat it so fast. In the relatives' house Grandmama and I slept in the same bed. I threw up in the middle of the night and they changed the linen. When I wanted to cut another thin slice, the knife slipped into my finger. I could see inside my finger. But then the blood came out and started to flow, it flowed across my hand and dripped onto the plate, and still it kept flowing. I got up to go to the bathroom, and I felt I was about to fall down. But I didn't, only I couldn't feel my feet and hands, and my head felt much bigger and my finger didn't hurt; everything felt good, because the door opened and the tile floor slammed into me, the black-and-white squares, and

your great-great-grandfather, had books brought to him directly from Berlin and Vienna, even though he was only an innkeeper. Everything that's in this world is alive. The world itself may be imagined as the largest living animal, because even a house, like everything else, is born, it lives and then dies, and that's all life is. This thought, of course, is more characteristic of the pantheists, like Bruno and Spinoza. But ultimately the idea is not alien to Hegel either, only his world is permeated not by the soul but by reason, the intellect." "Why are you filling his head with such nonsense again?" "That's why you must go on observing relentlessly, but don't get lost in details; systematize. However, don't ever think that your system is perfect, because above all systems stands God the Almighty." After they no longer lived upstairs, Grandmama thought I spent the afternoons in the garden, but I went up to the attic. The attic door was made of steel and creaked. This is where the ancestors lived whom Grandpapa had talked about. Once Csider came up here, too. We stepped carefully so they wouldn't hear us downstairs. If we climbed on the rafters, he could somehow pull up and move aside a roof tile and we could look out and see the garden. I couldn't pull up the tile by myself; Csider figured it out. He said that we should look in the crates. The crates were nailed shut. He said that if his father was a spy and was in touch with my father, and if they kept their secret documents in these crates, then we would expose them. My dog was sniffing the grass among the trees. He wasn't yet dead at that time. But we didn't find the documents. The candlestick was there, the one that almost fell on Grandpapa's head when he was walking on the street. I recognized it because Grandpapa had told me how it banged onto the sidewalk in front of him and when he picked it up he saw it had been dented pretty badly, and when he looked up he saw a man leaning out the fifth-floor window. The man shouted to beg Grandpapa's pardon and asked him to come upstairs if he wouldn't mind. Grandpapa did go upstairs, taking the candlestick with him, and then he asked to keep it as a souvenir. The one who leaned out the window was Frigyes, I called him Uncle Frigyes, and God not only saved Grandpapa's life but also presented him with a good friend. Uncle Frigyes told him that he had recently married, but that his wife always made him so angry he could hardly contain himself. Even when they were engaged they had lots of fights, but they thought things would improve after the wedding. He wanted to throw the candlestick at his wife, that's how angry he was at that moment, but luckily the candlestick flew out the window and luckily it hadn't killed Grandpapa. His wife had locked herself in the bedroom and was weeping. But he hoped that soon she'd get over it and, as the lady of the house, would invite Grandpapa for lunch. If Grand-

been to their house, too, but ghosts are white, Gábor said, not black. Éva came in from the garden and said that if we let her play with the disks she wouldn't tell her mother that we'd taken a look at the cream bottle in the bedroom. She had spied on us and seen it. In the evenings their mother always left the house because she had her shows to do. Once they asked me to come over after bedtime. I waited until Grandpapa and Grandmama went to sleep. I had to climb out the window because Grandmama took the key out of the lock. At home their mother didn't sing, only played the piano. In the evening a fellow came for her in a car. "Always some foreign car in front of their house!" Grandmama said. Standing at the window I too could see the car, its red lights were pretty in the dark. With Grandmama we went into town to buy new sandals. I outgrew the old ones. "Go in a cab! Take a cab!" Grandpapa shouted. Grandmama didn't want to. Grandpapa ordered the cab over the telephone. It was very hot. In the cab I kicked off my sandals so they wouldn't hurt. But as soon as we turned the corner Grandmama made the cabbie stop; I had to look for my sandals under the seat, and the cabbie was yelling furiously, "What the fuck are you jerking me around for?" We had to get out. Grandmama gave the man some money, but he went on yelling, "Old slut!" We took the bus into town. I was forbidden to talk about this. Grandmama got into a fight with the bus con-

narrow that he can't get into it, and in front of the door he has to take off his self and leave it outside along with his coarse robe. And in place of the neglected and humiliated little body it is the boundless soul that's groping in space, and when this nothing finds its nothing, the mouth exclaims, It's there, it's above me! He's lying! Above me! He's lying! So where is God, if not in the body and not in the soul? Does He exist at all?" "Grandmama says He does." "Oh, come on! Grandmama! Surely she must know? Ask her, has she ever talked to Him? Once, after a very long spiritual dry spell a saint asked God, Where have you been until now, O Lord? and God answered, *Within you!* Oh yes, but if you're looking for Him within, then He's outside, and if you're looking for Him outside, then He's within. *Dazwischen*, always *dazwischen*! Remember that well! Not body and not spirit, yet body as well as spirit. God's countenance is to be sought in innocence, not in pride and not in humility. While you guard your own innocence. If you yield to the body, it will take over, spread over your life like a cancer, you'll drown in your pride. If you yield to the spirit, it will take over, spread over your life like a cancer, you'll drown in your humility. I am free. I say, Long live the body! But I am also a thinker, and I say, Long live the spirit! Old as I am, when my body and my soul have had their day. I am a freethinker! I deny Him, curse Him, besmirch Him with my obscenities. I am not a believer. Still, He is always here because I think. Everything, everything disappears, save this word. And the word exists, therefore He exists, too, He who is designated by the word. If I could finally end this continuous thinking, the word would disappear and He would cease to exist, too. But where would He disappear to? And where would I be myself? Where would I be without my thoughts? Whither shall I go from thy spirit? or whither shall I flee from thy presence? If I ascend up into heaven, thou art there: if I make my bed in hell, behold, thou art there. Should I tell you the story of the suit? When arriving at the real questions, when it should really make an effort, the mind, incapable of thinking, tries to soothe itself with little anecdotes, you see? Well, I'll tell you the story anyway. But I warn you, don't look for edification here. Stories are nonrecurring details of life that offer no lessons to be learned. You can only find *inzwischen*, always between two stories, between two breaths: *dazwischen*!" I was scared because Grandpapa was yelling very loudly. "The story of my suit had to do with our family getting ready to go to the summer resort of Abbazia. Summer. In those days, schoolboys wore short pants with kneesocks. Those days are gone. But shorts with hairy legs like these? And what if we have to visit someone? I'd have been a laughingstock. My legs were good and hairy by that time because God blessed me with powerful natural

would have liked me to be Béla Zöld's wife, people even said that it wasn't me but my mother who was in love with Béla Zöld, but Father kept yelling that if I married a Protestant he'd burn a cross into my body, I must know forever where I belonged, he'd chase me naked across the village, but that's not what I want to tell you, even though all my problems started with that, but that's not what I want to tell you about, but the book we got from the priest, and it was full of legends, things that really happened, on the cover of it there was this large angel with its wings spread, about to fly up to heaven, and these were the legends I told the people in the village." When she thought I was already asleep, Grandmama would go back to her room but without closing the door. At night, if I woke up, I saw her standing by the window. She said she was sure that if she hadn't fallen asleep that night, Grandpapa wouldn't have died, and now it was her punishment that she couldn't fall asleep, she had to wait for the hour of Grandpapa's death, because every night she had to go and bring Grandpapa back, because sometimes she thought he hadn't died and the whole thing was only a prank. One night I woke up and Grandmama was standing in the middle of my room wearing the green velvet dress from which I had cut out the lead disks, and something was shining in her hair. She was coming toward me, had her arms stretched out, she was very angry and slapped me in the face, and I felt she had something hard in her hand, only I couldn't see what, it was so dark, but the slap didn't hurt. In town we were walking in the street and Grandmama was very beautiful because she was wearing her white hat and the silk dress with the black-on-white pattern. She said that all these houses had been destroyed during the war, all of them, and everybody died. I asked if we had also died, but she said no, because we were alive, weren't we? But where was I then, when I was not yet alive? Grandmama started yelling: "Feri! Feri! There goes your father! He can't hear me! Feri!" We were running. Lots of people were coming in our direction and lots of them were ahead of us. "Feri!" Grandmama was running ahead of me, I was behind her, but I couldn't see where my father was among all the people. People stopped, turned around, looked at us, and we were running among them. "Feri! My dearest little Feri!" I didn't recognize his back because I was looking for a uniform. "Feri!" He didn't have his cap on, either. We just looked at him. "What are you two doing here, Mother?" But he wasn't smiling, he just asked her. "He outgrew his sandals!" I looked at my sandals, which pinched my feet. My father hugged Grandmama, then kissed her, and then hugged and kissed me, too. His face was smooth and he didn't stink. He put his hand on my neck, and Grandmama held on to his arm. His palm felt good on my neck. That's how we were, waiting for a streetcar and two cars to pass. He came even closer. "And you're here, in town! And haven't even called?" "Come on, Mother, let's go to that pastry shop." "My God, why couldn't you phone? Why didn't you come home? Did Papa offend you in any way? Or did I?" The streetcar squeaked and its bell was ringing, because we ran across the street anyway, without waiting for it to pass. "Why didn't you come home, if you're here already? Feri!" In the pastry shop I got ice cream in a glass. Grandmama also asked for ice cream but didn't touch it, she was crying. And Father was angry. "Please, Mother, don't make a scene, I beg you. You know very well." "Yes, I do. I know everything. Everything, I know everything." "Please, Mother, stop it, you know what the situation is now. I can never be sure. You know. You know that's the kind of job I have. I can't talk about it. Be glad we've met, and I'd like to be glad about it, too." "I should be glad." "Please wipe your eyes. I've got no time, I've got to go somewhere, I'm in a hurry. It's trouble enough that we've met." "Trouble? Even meeting you like this is trouble?" "Yes, because instead of being glad to see me, you sit there crying. Mother, why not make good use of the little time we have, tell me the news from home. Is Papa all right? You still have some money left? Should I send more? Why don't you answer me? Mother, I haven't time for this sort of thing. Why don't you say

Lots of people were smoking. Grandmama said, Let's go, but I started crying and said I didn't want any shoes. "I can't get up." Grandmama pressed her hand to her chest. "I can't get up." She tried to get up but couldn't. In the meantime, my ice cream had melted. Again everybody was watching us, and a man next to us asked Grandmama, "Can I be of help, madam? Are you all right?" I tried to help Grandmama, but she couldn't get up. "I'm scared." Everybody was talking in the pastry shop. "I'm scared. I don't know why, I just am. There's nothing wrong, I'm just scared." The man took Grandmama's arm. "Do you feel ill, madam? A glass of cold water, maybe a glass of cold water?" He told the waiter to bring a glass of water and make it really cold. At night, whenever Grandmama would start to breathe hard, the way Grandpapa used to, I immediately took her some water. The waiter was bringing the water and also shouting, asking the honored guests if there was a doctor among them, because in the meantime Grandmama started to slide off her chair. "I'm a nurse!" The woman who said that got hold of Grandmama and splashed some of the water on her forehead, and everybody was standing around us. Grandmama's mouth was open. Grandmama had tied up Grandpapa's jaw with a kerchief. The nurse kept shouting that people should back off because Grandmama needed more air. "In this terrible heat!" Everybody had something to say. "They

her mother's dress. We threw pillows at one another. The door opened and their mother walked across the room, naked. In the other room she turned on the radio and put on her robe. She looked at herself in the mirror while listening to the radio. She said she was sure that now they would hang them all because the whole thing was nothing but a big sham. When Éva and I stopped dancing I felt a sharp pain in my side. Gábor couldn't get up. He grabbed a chair, pulled himself up, but slid back down, and his head was nodding all the time. Éva was laughing. Gábor threw up on the carpet. Éva quickly took off her mother's dress and ran out of the room. She had no panties on. When their mother left they'd close the windows and curtains and turn on the chandeliers. Éva would put on some dress. Gábor would put on a record and turn up the volume all the way. He'd take the sword off the wall and start fencing. Once he slashed one of the overstuffed chairs, ripping the velvet. Éva came up with the idea of hanging my dog. Gábor went to look for a rope. We started calling the dog. Clothes were drying on the rope in the garden. He cut it down with the sword. He stood on a chair and tied the rope to the chandelier. We called and called, but the dog wouldn't come. I had to clean up the vomit from the carpet. I could see everything he ate. They said they'd hang me instead. When the lawn was cut we had to rake the grass into a stack. We climbed to the top of the stack. Gábor played Eugénie Cotton, I was Pak Den Aj. We wrestled and I let him beat me because Eugénie Cotton was president of the International Women's League, and Pak Den Aj only president of the Korean Women's Coalition. We turned somersaults. Éva squealed and made a grab at the rope. The chandelier fell out of the ceiling. I didn't dare go home. Among the bushes I waited for something to happen. Csider called me over to their house to try the new swing his father had just set up. He showed me that standing up on it he could go really high. But he flew out of the swing, crashed through the window into the room. His mother came over to see Grandmama and I couldn't convince her that it wasn't me who'd done it. Grandmama was shouting in the garden. I thought maybe she'd found the Nina Potapova textbook which we kept in our apartment in the bushes. But it was my dog she'd found there. Together we took the dog into the house. "Somebody must have poisoned it." Grandmama dug a deep hole. Grandpapa also came out when we buried it.

ing the wind. But the ground should have been dug, it was autumn, the flowers were dried up, and my dog wasn't lying there any more; in his place the ground was hard and a little greasy, and there were a few hairs, small tufts of hair were left there that I should have plowed under, but somebody was still yelling, "Don't dig up the ground!" The wind hurled the voice at me: "Don't dig up the ground!" I wanted to put back the shovel. The window was banging. I started to run, but it was difficult in the deep snow. I ran along the wall of the house, but it was still hard to lift my feet in the thick snow, and it was cold, very cold, and the wind knocked snow into my face. I would have liked to look up to see finally where I was, but I couldn't because the sky was so bright! Down here it was completely dark. If only I could look up at the bright sky! But I had to close my eyes. In the dark. If only I knew what I should do! Then night fell. The next day, when I woke up and went out into the garden, two white butterflies were chasing each other. I ran after them, to see what butterflies do. They were fluttering around each other in glittering circles as they flew, and I ran after them, over the shrubs, over the hedges, out over the wide lawn, if only I had a butterfly net! and then vanished above a bush. Above the bush I couldn't follow them. The sky was blue, clear, and the light blinded me, as if it had sucked up the white glittering of the butterflies. And the silence. The bushes were there, squat and heavy. Hawthorn. Lilac. Elder. Hazel. Not far from the tree where one leaf sometimes stirred, even with no wind blowing. Through the secret passage I crawled under the bushes. In the nursery the bed was nicely made, with hay, good and soft. In the kitchen the pots were up on the shelf. A book lay on the rickety garden chair. I could hear my own panting. The soft haybed was tempting me to lie down and go to sleep, as though I was the child and the two of them had gone to the party, but I couldn't lie down because I kept hearing my own panting as if an animal, some kind of animal, was panting in the bushes, not me, and I could see it. I grabbed the shelf and yanked it out from under the pots, and the pots rattled and clanked, rolling into the bushes, and then for a moment I didn't hear my panting, but then I heard it again. This animal is panting right here, in the bushes! A dog. It was barking. It was scrabbling around, turning everything topsy-turvy. I ripped the haybed apart, lobbed the pots over the fence, and enjoyed hearing each and every thud as they landed; I dragged the garden chair out on the lawn, jumped on it, let the caning rip! let it tear, hang in shreds, the whole chair in smithereens; I tore out the pages of Nina Potapova and tossed its cover into the shrub, where it caught on a branch. I crawled back in, and the dog was barking and panting, its tongue hanging out. The dog was glad that it had finally demol-

cool and full of Grandmama's smell. On the night table a glass of water. On Grandmama's finger the ring
with the turquoise stone, the one I will inherit when
Grandmama dies. Carefully, so the floor wouldn't
creak, I left for the garden. The sun was always shining. I picked up a fallen peach and split it in two. Its
juice trickled down my fingers, a white worm was
inching its way over the wet pit. I pressed the worm
into the meat of the peach. It wiggled, struggled, but
I pushed it so far into the soft wet mass that I couldn't
see it, and then quickly, worm and all, I popped the
peach into my mouth, and careful not to bite down, I
swallowed the whole thing. I imagine the worm got to
my stomach alive. Now it's down there in the dark,
it's alive and has no idea where it is. And still it wasn't
evening. Bees arrived. I felt something was wrong with
me. Suddenly. It was as if somebody else were sitting
in the grass, somebody whose heaviness I could feel,
but it wasn't me, and everything was hazy, blurred.
Suddenly. A small shred of a cobweb glistened and
disappeared in the air. And whatever else I looked at,
it wasn't I who was seeing it, that's why everything
was disappearing, and I could never tell what it was
I'd just seen a moment before, because I could no
longer see it. And I'm sure it's like this only with me,
and that's why I must be bad. But I must keep this
from others and pretend I see everything they see. And
I wasn't sitting where I had sat before, but jumped up

I thought of going into the house and telling Grand-mama, but my body started moving on its own and I rolled down the slope; sky, grass, trees, ground, sky, grass, and bushes spinning closer and closer, and all the while I was shouting, I'm lying on blades of grass! lying on blades of grass! and each time I rolled to the ground it shut me up and that felt good. And then the clear sky again, and the shrubs that gave me shade, and the white flowers, too, and I could keep my eyes open and look at things without knowing whether they were close or far away. I should bring a ball to play with. The red ball flew up into the sky. The heavy white calyxes swung gently at the end of the upward-reaching branches. A bee came. It landed on the rim of the cup, strolled around it, then crawled inside, a humming shade on the petals. At dusk the flowers folded up. Down by the fence, as if it were raining huge white drops in the night, falling from somewhere but never reaching the ground. A face among the leaves. But I didn't know whose. Slowly, as if in pain, the man opened his mouth, wanting to say something, but it was very dark inside the mouth and something I couldn't see was moving in that darkness. And all his efforts were in vain. Then he reached out and plucked a flower. He showed it to me, his mouth still open. He wanted me to smell it. I could see inside the flower, but the water inside it flowed out, all at once just spilled out of the flower. "Why did you roll the

laughed because I remembered how the man had kept stuffing the covers into his mouth. A bird landed on the branch above my head; it lifted its pointed tail feathers a little and a white limy discharge dribbled down on the leaf where the frog was sitting. Bird shits lime! That too I had to laugh at. The bird turned its head every which way and took off. I wanted to see where it was flying to. I ran among the bushes, leaves and branches knocked against my face, and I could see it flying over to Éva and Gábor's house to have a drink. I heard something crack. An empty snail shell. Thick ivy with dark leaves was growing everywhere under the bushes. In the meantime, the bird flew on, over the house. On the terrace where their mother always yelled for them, a large sunshade, folded around its long pole, had been leant against the railing. Here, the garden seemed even brighter. Here, too, the shrubs were set in a circle around the neatly cut lawn and, in the middle, the calm water of the pool. The tub was floating on the water. I thought that somebody must have stayed in the house after all and was watching me from behind the closed shutters. Maybe I should say that my ball had rolled over here? Every move made a noise. But the shutters did not move, and nobody came out on the terrace, either. I kept listening. Maybe they had a pistol and would shoot me, and all I'd done was to come to look for my ball. It seemed the house was already covered with dust. Still, there must be somebody in there. The barrel of the weapon in the cracks of the shutter. But really, I'm only looking for my ball, honestly, because it was dark when it flew over here and I couldn't find it. Go ahead, look for it! I stepped out of the bushes. If there's nobody in the house, then the whole place belongs to me. I'll move in and everything will be mine. I can sit down at the piano. The sword is mine, too. The rifle above the fireplace and the little picture that glows in the dark—they're mine, too. And the Japanese picture. If they didn't take it with them. And I shall take me a wife and we shall live here. And my wife will wear their mother's dresses, and I shall bring over the green velvet dress I wanted to give to Éva. In the evening a car will come for us, its red light shining bright, and she will put on the green velvet dress to go to the party. The jewels! I know, she showed me, I know where they are! I started to move, pretending to be looking for something in case somebody was watching me from the house, if they had come back, so they could see I was looking for my ball. But I couldn't go on with this game because I couldn't shake the thought that I knew, that they had showed me where the jewels were stashed; and the piano, and the Japanese picture, and the sword, and the rifle. Maybe I should tell them I had left my ball there, in case somebody was in the house after all. What kind of ball? Red, with big white dots. They probably didn't know

silence down here all around me somehow settled into me. Gábor and Éva could never wait like this; only I can. Which means they're not here. There is nobody up there. Nobody. I propped my hand against the crate, my eyes became accustomed to the dark. The long passage takes a turn under the house. I had to stop and wait after each step, until I didn't hear my footsteps, and then, with my palms on the wall, to prepare my next step. Rough mortar sticking out between the bricks. My feet still hadn't bumped into the bottom of the staircase. Another step on the coarse concrete floor. Another feel of the hands, another step. At last the stairs, and on top of the stairs the door. It's open a crack. Without creaking, the crack widens silently. But the hallway is dark. Warm and musty. Through the crack of the door the hallway smell rolls out, that smell! Though the cold air of the cellar is cooling my back, I am hot, and my inner heat and this outer cold touch my skin at the same time; I shudder. Something rustles among the dark leaves and tangled runners. A dull glitter under two leaves. Smoothly the snake propels itself forward as if swimming on the surface of water. Toward me. And I can't tell where it starts or where it ends, I can only see the glistening of its light brown body under the leaves as it tranquilly propels itself toward me. Then it stiffens into motionlessness. Its gaping mouth and two clever eyes among the leaves. It seems to be staring forward, toward its destination, but in the meantime it sees me as well. Closing its mouth, it too stops breathing. On its steely head darker and thicker scales. Its nose is two holes under the eyes. It could pass for a tendril among the leaves. Stupid little snake. The sun is hitting your head. I couldn't slap or hit it fast enough, it would slip out from under my hand, like a lizard. If I stretched only my arm toward it, not even the shadow would reach it, because the sun shines on both of us from the front, throwing the shadows behind us. I extend my arm very very slowly, so slowly that I can't notice it myself. I must grab it from behind, by the neck. It keeps looking at me, unsuspecting. The body is motionless among the leaves, but its end cannot be seen. I unlock my knees just a hair, to get even closer, and stay that way. As far as I can tell it has made no move at all, must not be thinking about protecting itself. I've got to reach it from behind so it can't bite and squirt the poison into my hand. This last move must be made very quickly, but I don't know how. Now it seems as though it can see what I'm doing, after all; still, it keeps staring ahead, unsuspecting, in the direction it had been moving, toward the pool, yet it appears to be looking at me as well. I am growing weak and tired, but I do want to do it. I can't bend my knees any more or bring my arm any closer. The tiniest rustling sound and I pounce, and I feel its steely head between my fingers, its body is thrashing, my hold on it is clumsy, whose blood it was, the snake's or mine, on the concrete around the crushed head, and my hand was like the snake's smashed head, as if I were still squeezing and hitting it, but it no longer hurt. I couldn't, I just couldn't get up. The snake was writhing on the dry concrete. I ran. I tripped on something and I couldn't run, but I couldn't fall either; still, I should have been glad it wasn't coiled around my arm any more, but my arm, my fingers kept feeling its body; at last I stumbled and fell down. It felt good to lie on the grass. I was cooling my hand on the grass. It was throbbing. But I couldn't lie on the grass because all the other snakes would be crawling out, coming after me, I had to get up. I felt that the way things were I could never go home again. Silence reigned in the garden except for my own panting. They'd be crawling out from under the bushes. I knew if I looked back it would still be writhing. I'll stay here and nobody will know about it. I let the iron window stay slightly ajar to let in a bit of light. I started walking down the corridor, but it was dark. I groped for the steps. The door was locked. I was sitting in the crate. We had lined the crate with old rugs to make it soft. Outside, the sun was shining, a piece of empty sky. My thigh and my leg cooled my hand. I wondered what would happen if the poison from the snake's mouth had dripped into my bruised hand. I'll die right here in this crate. The blood was becoming gooey, probably because of the poison. I would have loved to fall asleep in the crate, but the poison was stinging my hand. I didn't look, I didn't want to see! I washed my hand at the garden faucet so I wouldn't be bloody if I died, so nobody would know what happened to me. I was sitting in the crate, just staring; outside, the sun was shining. But I had to get out of here, too: even bigger snakes were crawling out of the corner. If the door hadn't been locked I could have taken the sword off the wall and slashed the snake to pieces so it wouldn't wriggle any more. A big green lizard was lying on the ground, on its back, still kicking, but I poured a bunch of pebbles over it and I was frightened, even though it was barely alive. I had to get out of here, too. When I wanted to crawl out of the cellar I saw Csider walking up the terrace steps. I wanted to see what he was doing. He looked in through the glass door. Kicked the pole of the sunshade. It slid along the railing and with a huge bang fell on the stone floor of the terrace. Csider looked around, without moving, listening, to see if anybody was around. He started down the stairs. I quickly pushed out the cellar's iron window and it creaked. "Hey, Csider!" He saw it was only me. In the summer his hair was always close-cropped. He rubbed his head, pretending he wasn't scared. I stayed in the cellar, the bricks wobbling under my feet, but I didn't want him to see my hand. "Can I get in there?" He bent down and looked in. "What's there?" "From here

afraid he might find the matches and the candle, and I shouldn't have mentioned them, either. "And what's it like?" "Well, completely naked, and it's hairy down there. And she was walking around like that, and we were right there." "Hey, Simon, do you have any paper here?" "Paper? I'm sure there's paper upstairs. But they put a lock on the door. We should open it somehow." Csider came over to me. "Shut up! I told you not to yell!" I couldn't see his face because the sun was shining outside. He was whispering. "I was never friendly with them, not me!" "We should get something to open the door with! They have a picture that glows in the dark. Japanese. And they told me, they showed me where the jewels are! And the sword!" "Sword?" "Come on, Csider, let's do it!" "What?" "What we did in our attic!" "Nah, not now, now I gotta take a shit." He walked into the corner and pulled down his pants. Squatted on his haunches. I kept looking at him. The shit was coming out of him. He squatted there for a long time, and now and then he moaned a little.

hand and drag me along and I couldn't see anything among the people because they'd be trying to squeeze me out, and Grandmama would be yelling, too: "Shameless creatures! Can't you see I have a child with me?" "You should have sent your maid!" "This lout she calls a child!" "Why didn't you leave him at home?" "In a white hat! She always wears a white hat when they're selling lard." Grandmama would tear the white hat off her head and everybody could see she was almost completely bald, and then we'd be served right away. Grandmama told me that one particular saleswoman cheated everybody and that her blond hair was dyed. Once, this saleswoman started to scream: "Oh! Oh my God!" She was flailing her arms, banging all over the place with her hands and screaming, "Ohmygod!" and stamping her feet. "Get out of here! All of you! Oh my God, why don't you all shut up! Or get out of here! I'm a working woman! I can't work like this! I can't count like this! I've got to keep track! I can't bear this! I can't stand it! I'll just stop, that's all! I can't stand it!" Everyone fell silent. She cut the lard with a huge knife and slapped it on a sheet of paper, and everybody kept quiet. She threw the paper on the scale and cut some more and smeared it on the paper again and watched the scale. She was crying. We were standing right up front. The woman went on cutting the lard and crying; she'd wipe her eyes and her face got all greasy and all we heard was her crying as if afraid of somebody. The long knife in her hand. "Don't be angry with me, please! I can't bear it! I can't bear it! Don't be angry with me!" The man I'd seen in church was stroking her dyed blond hair. "Please, calm down! Nobody's angry with you. We're all human beings." But then somebody said the man was comforting the woman only because he wanted to get his lard out of turn, and then everybody started shouting again. The fish kept opening its mouth, moving its gills, swimming around in the tub. Grandmama said we'd eat it on Friday. I pictured the image of the crucifix. The hammer, the pliers, the saw and nails were kept in a drawer in the hallway, under the mirror. I looked at my palm, but I didn't dare drive a nail into it. The fish was swimming as if looking for an exit. During a single round of the tub it opened its gills four times. Grandpapa asked me if I wanted to hear the story of the girl who smelled like a fish. "Yes." "Well, listen, then," Grandpapa said, "so you'll know what's what!" We were looking at the fish. "Everything in this story happened a very long time ago, and very far from here." I thought he meant the time of the ancestors he'd told me about up in the attic, but Grandpapa shook his head. "No! Didn't I ask you to listen? You're not paying attention! Our ancestors have had no time even to die, and they're still alive, they live here, within us. But the story I'm about to tell you happened in times we've already forgotten, when giant

by yourself. Well then, some time after the creation, which means a long time ago and far away, there lived a river, the great river, what kind of river? back then people didn't call rivers by names! but later it had a nickname—Ganga—and on the shore of this river there lived a heavenly fairy. And now the tale begins. Her hair was black as night, her eyes radiant like the surface of the water in the brightest hour, her skin smooth silk. And that's how the heavenly fairy lived, rejoicing in her own beauty. Not far from the river: a thick forest. There, where even the sunshine couldn't penetrate, in eternal dimness, nourishing his old body with grass and snakes, lived a saintly man. Mortal, but as pure in his saintliness as was the heavenly fairy in her beauty, as pure as a mortal could possibly be. He never felt desires, therefore he was never driven by hatred or love. An incurious being, a crystal of existence, a crystalline soul locked in perishable flesh. And the days of the flesh were numbered. The flesh was waiting for death, the flesh of the heart, the flesh of the stomach still digesting berries, the thin membranes, the walls of the veins all waiting to die. There, in the depth of the dark forest. Because where the hell else should a saint await death if not in the depth of the dark forest? That's what tales are like. Now he had only a few hours left. He knew that once these days, months, or hours were over, he would return his sensate body and insensate soul to the lap of the one in-

and caught the beautiful little fish. He put the fish in his knapsack and took it home. To kill it, he knocked it on the head, just as I will knock this one in a minute. Cut open its stomach to clean out all the dirty innards. But look at this! The beautiful fish had no innards. Two tiny children were cowering in its belly. One was fashioned to be a little boy, the other one was a little girl. The fisherman was very scared and sent for the king. The king examined the signs, being well versed in such matters, and said, You and I are lucky, because spirit gives birth to spirit, even down to seven generations, and because this spirit chose to divide its immortality in two, we can share it. I'll take the boy with me and raise him. You take care of the girl, she is yours. And in two days the girl grew up and she was beautiful. Her hair black as night, her eyes radiant like the surface of the water in the brightest hour, her skin smooth silk. Still, she didn't have any suitors, because she smelled bad, like a fish. Every sentence is the setting for the jewel of wisdom! Are you listening? Pay close attention to this! The spirit, when it crawls into a body, becomes smelly! That's the meaning of the curse! But let's get quickly to the end of this, so you can hold the whole fruit in your hand. The fisherman let the girl work as a ferry woman. She took people back and forth across the river. The passengers were dazzled by her, but they couldn't touch her. Many years went by, but the girl was not getting old. What was she like after so very many years?" Grandpapa raised his finger. This meant I had to learn by heart what he was about to say. He also raised his fingers when he rattled off the seven cardinal sins. "Because of the seven sins God has withdrawn into the seventh heaven. Why? Come on! Tell me! Why?" "Because the serpent tempted Adam and Eve into the sin of pleasure. And God withdrew into the first heaven." "Go on!" "Because the sin of envy deprived Cain of his humanity and he murdered his own brother." "Who was he?" "Abel. And God withdrew into the second heaven." "Go on!" "Because Enoch and his companions fell into the sin of idolatry." "And God?" "Withdrew into the third heaven." "What do we call idolatry?" "When people worship not the Creator but His creations!" "What do we call God's creations?" "I don't know." "What do you mean you don't know? Think! You know everything! There's no such thing as 'I don't know'! Know then: God's creation includes everything that exists in heaven and on earth, in the known and the unknown world, and also everything that does not exist. Go on! Continue!" "Continue what?" "Noah's time is next!" "People in Noah's time were guilty of the sin of cruelty, and they were unworthy. And God withdrew into the fourth heaven. King Amraphel, wallowing in the sin of injustice, oppressed other peoples who had never harmed him. For this, God withdrew into the fifth heaven." "Why did he withdraw into the sixth?" "King Nimrod built a tower." "In Babylon. Why?" "Because he wanted to reach all the way up to heaven!" "And what's that?" "The sin of ambition!" "Finish the list of sins!" "And God was already looking at us from the sixth heaven because a king had taken from Abraham, who was formerly Abram, one of his wives, thus committing a sin against family happiness." Grandpapa wanted me to learn everything that he knew. Together we repeated: "Her hair black as night, her eyes radiant like the surface of the water in the brightest hour, her skin smooth silk." Grandpapa laughed, glad that I already knew the words, and he shouted, "That's what a beautiful woman is like! But let's hear what happened. A beautiful woman is beautiful even after a thousand years! A thousand years later a wise old man came to the river. The woman who smelled like fish was taking him across. It was the spirit that made her immortally beautiful, the spirit which, as we know, smells foul when inside a body. The wise man began pleading with her that she should gratify him when they reached the other side. But this is how the girl answered him: Lots of people live on the shore of the river, fishermen and hermits. You want me to love you right before their eyes? The wise man raised his finger and fog descended over the whole region. And the powerful old man was snickering under his beard at how quickly he had outsmarted the girl! But this is

smelling girl, the clever one, had only one wish: that her body not smell like a fish. And she received him. At the spot where she received him she remained fish-smelling. On the same day she gave birth to Vyasa. And on the same day Vyasa matured into a lovely youth and asked his mother to leave him to himself, for having conquered the tyranny of the body, he would like to devote his life to God. The girl was left all alone, just as the saint in the forest had promised. She married one of the fishermen, became a woman like the rest of the girls, gave birth like the others, seven times, her breasts drooped, wrinkles invaded her lips, and she died. It was Vyasa who continued to live the life of the fairy which his grandmother had planted into his mother and his father had passed on to him. That's what the fairy tale tells us." "And is this true?" I asked. Grandmama was calling out that we should bring the fish. The fish was calmly swimming around the tub, not knowing what would happen to it if we took it to Grandmama. And when I asked Grandpapa what his grandfather was like, he didn't answer me. It was so dark in his eyes, no matter how hard I looked I couldn't see what was in them. I thought he would start shouting. When he shouted for a long time his mouth went black. But he only raised his finger: "The time has come!" And he looked at me as if he were searching for something in me. And slowly he laid his hand back on the armrest of his chair. With its fingers open the hand rested on the maroon velvet. As if it were not a hand but a strange animal. Sometimes I would touch the thick veins. While he was asleep. "Put your hand on my head." He was whispering. His hair was soft and white. I didn't understand. He gave me a look and then lowered his lids. A vein was bulging on his white temple, too; once, on a map, he'd shown me what a winding and twisting river the Jordan was. My hand became warm on his head. He was whispering: "The time has come! I can see it. Your mind is opening up to the idea of time. I can see it. And that's a great thing. Let's help with the opening of the gates, shall we?" He was nodding, and gave me a nice smile, and opened his eyes and pressed me to his chest. "Help me get up!" But I couldn't help him, because he was hugging me, and I saw from very close the little pores on his nose, full of little specks of dirt which I had never noticed before. I thought he was going to cry and then I would see from this close where the tears were coming from, but he yelled and I could see into his mouth. "Help me get up!" But I couldn't help him. "Give me my stick!" While I was looking for his stick, Grandpapa held on to the chair, though he could walk even without his stick. Grandpapa was very large. When he got up it seemed the room wouldn't be big enough for him. The walls came closer. He was walking with his stick, and he was yelling, "The time has come!" But I didn't understand and had no idea where

you won't see my face." And he didn't say anything more. I thought we'd have a quiet time just thinking about things. Our shoes in the dust. He was breathing hard in the heat. I was afraid, I didn't know what might happen. And everything was rather dim, and the roof tiles were making little crackling sounds, and Grandpapa was breathing, and above our heads the sun shone through the window, but I couldn't see the sky, only the light as it was falling, slanted and never-ending, into the attic. I didn't know what could possibly be happening to Grandpapa's face that I wasn't allowed to see and yet I had to stay there. Just keep sitting together. Grandmama always cleaned Grandpapa's yellow shoes and brushed them till they shone brightly. Maybe I'd have to tell him again what I was thinking about, but I didn't know what I was thinking, and I wasn't allowed to say I didn't know, but I really didn't know. I would have liked to stamp my feet on the floor, the attic had a strange hollow sound. In the attic I could feel the house under me, yet it was like not being in the house. With a long stick I poked at the dim, dark corners. Before I'd settle in one, let other creatures get out. By the time I turned my head in their direction they disappeared. Gone behind my back. I could see their color, like the dust of the attic: gray. They were crouching at the foot of the beams or standing by the chimney. When I came with the stick they seemed about to scream, they opened their mouths and vanished. Always getting behind my back. Once, when I turned to see where one of them had disappeared to, and spun around so fast it wouldn't have time to scurry away, it was hanging on the rope off a beam because it had hanged itself, and its skin had already dried and stuck to its bones, or maybe it was like that all the time, but then it disappeared, too. Grandpapa was breathing slowly, but his forehead was sweaty, and he sat all doubled up and his eyes were closed, as if he had fallen asleep. "Don't look at me!" I can't imagine how he could have seen me with his eyes shut. "When I was a child, we sat down on the bench in my grandfather's courtyard. Under the mulberry tree. Don't look at me! said my grandfather, just listen to what I'm about to tell you. My face must not interfere with your vision." I watched the light falling between the rafters and the motes undulating. "I leaned back against the trunk of the mulberry tree, taking care my grandfather didn't see this little impropriety, and I looked up into the leaves, each leaf separately; so many leaves! Occasionally a mulberry would plunk down. We settled on that bench because I asked my grandfather what his grandfather had been like, and then my grandfather said the time has come and made me sit on the bench. It was Sabbath, that is, Saturday, after lunch. For lunch we had cholent, the bean dish baked overnight in the home kiln, with fine, tender beef in it, and we also had sweet hominy, served cold. By the time my grandfather finished with everything I'm about to tell you now, the evening star had risen in the clear sky. But we kept on sitting there for a long time and saw the full moon, too, and it was red. My grandfather said he would be embarrassed if he couldn't begin what he wanted to tell me the way his grandfather had started his story. And his grandfather had also said he would be embarrassed if he couldn't begin his story the way his grandfather had begun his. And it began like this: you are a kohen, from the family of the high priest Aaron, which means nothing more and nothing less than as if I had said— and this is what my grandfather said to me and his grandfather had said to him—that you are one of the chosen group within the chosen people, the brother of Moses, the man whom God addressed thus, according to Scripture: And thou shalt speak unto all that are wise-hearted, whom I have filled with the spirit of wisdom, that they make Aaron's garments to consecrate him, that he may minister unto Me in the priest's office. Thus my grandfather's grandfather had quoted the words to him, and thus he quoted the words to me, as I am quoting the words to you, and that is how they opened the gate which I am opening for you now. Do you hear what I am saying? Because speaking this softly I cannot hear my own words, I can only feel them. If a deaf man speaks softly it's as if not he but his spirit were speaking. Right now, like this, all right?

stood the mulberry tree, was surrounded by this stone fence, and the store opened from there, not from the street. Very clever. If something should happen, it wouldn't be so easy to loot it. It was the grandfather who had come here from Nicolsburg who figured this out. In case something happened they could lock and bolt the gate. From the store you could go into the living room. That's where Grandfather sat with his books, in front of the window. I can still see it today. If anybody came, I can still hear the little door in the front gate, and then the little bell on the store door would ring, and Grandfather would call out from behind his book, telling the customer to take what he liked, just leave the money on the counter. Go on, pour for yourself, drink. But this didn't work too well because a lot of people cheated him. And Grandmother's counting and recounting the pennies didn't help much; Grandfather was going quite mad with his learning and yelling that he couldn't be bothered with oil and salt until he clarified for himself the existence of God. This is understandable! He would eat and rest only to gather the further strength needed to unlock the mystery of mysteries. And if he was working on the mystery of mysteries, how could they expect him to pour drinks for inebriated peasants? That's understandable! Well, isn't it? Grandmother understood, all right, but she pulled asunder what God had put together: the great conjugal bed. So long as he is wallowing in the sin of being a nonbeliever, so long as he refuses to take care of the store, he cannot touch me! I don't want his sins to be paid for by those who haven't even been conceived! The rabbi agreed with Grandmother, but he also wasn't angry with Grandfather. He told Grandmother it would be best to wait. That's how they continued to live together. For eight years no more children were born. They already had three. But eight years later Grandfather found the irrefutable arguments. And in the ninth year my father was born. Your father was born, the firstborn of my own faith, the one and only, my real son, my Joseph, the son conceived in the bliss of faith. That's how Grandfather said it under the mulberry tree, and we could already see the evening star in the sky, this sentence was the period at the end of his narrative, and then the moon rose, all red. But Grandfather, your great-great-grandfather, could not have known then what I, your grandfather, know now. He couldn't have known that the doubt germinating in him for eight years would grow ears, shoot up, and ripen in me, ready to be harvested; I couldn't have known this either when the red moon rose that evening. Though that, too, must have been a signal. What in him was only a doubt, in me turned into certainty. I couldn't have known then that I was coming into the world to carry out the law, to bring about destiny, and to guide the great river back to the place from which two thousand years ago it had set out to meander all over the world. I have to utter a single word which I wouldn't want to say. Jesus. Once, in 1598, one of your ancestors in Buda cried out like this: Let us die so that we may be saved. That has become my motto. You too will have to choose a motto, or it might choose you. To kill everything that has remained so that we may go on living! Kill it, so all this can turn into a dead myth. Because a savior was born, but the people did not notice. Only the punishment their inattention would bring upon them. For the Law, the Torah, says it very clearly: But if thou will not hearken unto the voice of the Lord thy God, cursed shalt thou be in the city, and cursed shalt thou be in the field. Cursed shall be thy basket and thy store. Cursed shall be the fruit of thy body, and the fruit of thy land, the increase of thy kine, and the flocks of thy sheep. Cursed shalt thou be when thou comest in, and cursed shalt thou be when thou goest out. The Lord shall make the pestilence cleave unto thee. And thou shalt grope at noonday, as the blind gropeth in darkness; and thou shalt not prosper in thy ways; and thou shalt be only oppressed and spoiled evermore, and no man shall save thee. And the Lord shall scatter thee among people which neither thou nor thy fathers have known, and there thou shalt serve other gods: even wood and stones. The curse! I have turned the curse into my life! That is why I have come. To fulfill the curse! Red was

the Lord hath heard me! And she gave birth to her son and she called his name Simeon, which means, having been heard. Just as the Lord had given the son into Leah's womb, so did the Lord put the son's name unto her lips. And that is the first seal. For this name, Simon or, more archaically, Simeon, has a double meaning, and the two are woven together; one of its meanings is, The bearer of the name will hear the voice of the Lord; its other meaning is, The Lord will hear the voice of the one entitled to this name. And what happens when someone breaks the seal of the name, like Leah's second son, who in his heedlessness did not hear the Lord? Leah's son wrought terrible, bloody vengeance on the inhabitants of Shechem after they had defiled Dinah. He took revenge on the innocent because the guilty ones had run away. And that was a sin! And the Lord avenged the sin with a curse—so that they shall remember! And He delivered Simeon and his tribe into servitude, into the hands of their own brethren. That is the second seal. That's how the Simons become servants, if only God's servants. That is the third seal. And six thousand years have gone by. And since that time this has been your name. But the gate is not quite open yet, there is only a slight crack but it's widening. Don't look at me! Just listen! I'm going on with the story."

only heard of each other—I do have a relative in Jerusalem, one would say, originally from faraway Cyrene, but I don't know him personally; and the other one knew this much, I do have a relative somewhere in Galilee, where he was a fisherman until he met this false prophet who for the last three years has been roaming around unpunished, dazzling the gullible multitudes with his miracles, until this charlatan told him, From henceforth thou shalt be a fisher of men, and took him on as his disciple, and who knows where they are now, that's what people have told me. The two Simons had never seen each other, though the Lord saw to it that a particular day, the fifteenth of Nisan, was a memorable one for both of them. They resembled each other, both in appearance and in their nature, as if the same mother had given birth to them; they were both short, gaunt, with burning dark eyes, and extremely taciturn. Those who knew them only casually could easily take one for the other. Look! Here comes Simon of Galilee, the disciple of the one whose name is not to be uttered, and how rich a garment he's wearing today, what magnificent sandals! Look, here he comes! Could this be Simon of Cyrene? But why the shabby garb, what garbage dump did he get his torn sandals from? The two Simons were not looking for each other. One was as rich as the other was poor. And each said to himself when thinking of the other, What have I got to do with him? That was

the firstborn. He loved Alexander even though the boy showed no signs that he could continue his father's pursuits; this boy knew nothing about money, had no idea what to buy and when, or how to sell at a profit; only the farmland held Alexander's interest, the way plants grew and animals were born; but this love of the land was still dearer to the father's eyes and heart than the tinkering of Rufus, the younger boy, who even as a small child would stand for hours in front of the workshops of gold- and silversmiths, watching them pound out their trays and pitchers, absorbed in the adroit movements with which they fit precious stones into ornaments to be worn on necks, hands, and feet. It was already the middle of the month of Iyar. People were quickly forgetting that someone had been crucified. Alexander harvested the barley from which the first sheaf would be part of the holiday sacrifice; the barley that year had a twentyfold yield, twenty seeds for every seed planted, which could be called a good average. The hot days were already ripening the wheat. But Simon cared for none of this. He couldn't step out of the house because the light hurt his eyes, and he no longer knew where this light was coming from or what it really was; the city's noise offended his ears, and if he had to mingle with the people jostling around the temple, who were so filthy and ignorant, he would have felt that everybody was looking at him and mocking him; Simon prayed, asking the Lord to enlighten his mind so that he might understand what was happening. Sometimes he would call for Alexander—the boy could not see his father in the dark—and ask him to go to the temple and inquire of Rabbi Abiathar if there was any news, but the rabbi's message was always the same: Nothing. Simon was lost in this nothingness. Within a few days he was found dead. Instead of feeling bereaved, Rufus was annoyed. While looking at his dead father he thought, We found him dead in the corner, like a dog. He went up on the roof, along the edge of which ran a wide carved stone balustrade and handsome columns supported a light shade against the sun—that was all the fashion in Jerusalem, but some thought it was a loathsome aping of the Romans, and as such deeply immoral: to block the light from our faces! thus, allegedly, grumbled Rabbi Abiathar himself— when he leaned on the stone balustrade, Rufus sometimes could see, on the shadeless roof of the neighboring house, the girl he loved and with whom the Lord would bring him together on the fifteenth of Nisan, the day that had proved so fateful for his father. And now he desired to see her more than ever before, because from now on he could love not only the proportions of her body, the sheen of her hair, and her awkward side glances, but also the fragrance of her breath, her voice, her fearful alarm, and her laughter. On the death day, the girl did not show. A mulberry fell on my grandfather's forehead. I didn't dare laugh, even though he smeared it all over his face. He always felt and knew everything. He said, Don't look! If you look, you can't listen, and a mulberry is no big thing." Quickly I turned my head because I also caught myself looking at Grandpapa. "That reminds me! To give you an idea what my grandfather was like! Once we were playing under the mulberry tree and the mulberries kept falling off the tree, and we made up a word game. Mulberry in Hungarian is *szeder*, which sounds like Seder, so we made up the song: The szeder tree burst into bloom on Seder eve! Seder-bloom the eveburst bloomszeder intotree! Szederburst treeve sederinto! Evetree on bloominto sederburst! Der evenszeder burst bloome in der sedtree! And we ran to Grandfather and asked him, DER EVENSZEDER BURST BLOOME IN DER SEDTREE—what does that mean? Grandfather laughed. *Ihr seid ja dumme Esel! Wir hatten dasselbe Spiel gemacht, als mein Grossvater diesen Baum setzte. Es ist ja ungarisch gesagt und heisst,* THE SEDER TREE BURST INTO BLOOM ON SZEDER EVE! Grandfather laughed and we were yelling and shouting, so happy that Grandfather knew everything but had gotten it mixed up, and we shouted, *Nein! Nein! Eben umgekehrt!* Just the opposite! ON SEDER EVE THE

* You are asses! We used to play that game when my grandfather planted this tree. It's Hungarian, and it means . . .

servants carrying the paschal lamb; she stops in the shade and, raising her hand to her forehead, softly calls up to her son: Rufus, please put on some decent clothes today! Rufus leans against a column, doesn't answer. He runs his finger across the stone, his fingers like the feel of the finely carved fluting. The clothes Rufus wears are not like his grandfather's, or his father's, or even his brother's. Rufus dresses according to the latest fashion: a white, light wrap, gathered and held in rich folds on one shoulder by an ornamental clasp; he himself made the clasp and fitted it with precious stones. He's also made the belt, which shows his slender waist as even narrower than it is. The garb is short, exposing not only one of his shoulders on top but also his well-formed knees, his shapely thighs and powerful legs, it's that short. The garb is elegant, but it also has a martial air; legionnaires wear something similar. In the motionless air the city is boiling. From here you can see the city wall and the Southern Gate, where groups of arrivals set up camp, stir up the dust. The sun is still in the sky, but the noise is increasing, because as soon as the sun sets the killing of lambs will begin all over the city. The eight-day holiday is about to commence in Jerusalem. Newcomers are looking for lodging, a courtyard where they might set up their tents. Word has it that during the night, at the head of a whole legion, Pilate had also come to town. For the skin of a lamb one can get lodging. Up on the roof, above the throng and the hubbub, Rufus feels himself more of an outsider than the poorest beggar. He believes this to be so because of his love, which nothing can assuage. But no! The roots of his love are sickly. It's not a wife he wants to take according to the Law, but, rather, he wants to possess beauty, to capture the elusive in the palpable. And what is taking place around him, below him, is so chaotic and coarse, so against his liking. Rachel, who in the company of her mother and sisters sometimes appears on the neighboring roof, is slender, yet her body is also round. The contrast of her slenderness, a sign of upward striving, and her roundness, the body's tendency to curve back onto itself, makes for a perfect shape, and that is what is driving Rufus on: his eyes are enjoying in the girl the same perfection that he manages to mold with his hands, with his fine little chisels and hammers, when making filigrees of silver or copper. And he finds this play of opposites in his own unclothed body, a sin which is no secret to his parents; his mother often spies on him and what she sees— though she finds the words with great difficulty—she relates to Simon. Proportions! In Jerusalem everything is governed by laws, but the laws are proportioned differently; the mind's rule over the senses, reason, not the rule of faith! and reason without the senses is disproportionate! In law it's logic that keeps the right proportions, and everything that falls out of the realm of the law's logic is filth, waste! A sense or feeling that begs to take tangible form is considered a disrespectful violation of the law! The lamb that one must slaughter after sundown but before darkness falls must be a yearling and a male; and that evening everywhere the meal, dedicated to the memory of a people's flight, must be consumed in haste, without enjoyment; to eat the lamb's blood is forbidden, it's a sin! You must not break its bones! Any member of the family who partakes not of the paschal meal, of the lamb and of the bitter herbs, partakes of death! For he has sinned! It's a sin! The next morning Rufus may again wear his fancy clothes. Today is the fifteenth of Nisan, that day. On the second day of Pesach let every man who harvests his own land bring a sheaf of first fruits for a temple offering! Rufus takes the sickle, Alexander brings the sheaf, and stepping smartly in front of them is their father, who is much shorter than they. Their land is outside the city, beyond the Northern Gate. Now they're coming back. Simon is silent, his sons are not talking either. The descent is steep from the bald rocky hilltop which, for this reason, people call Golgotha. In the hazy light past the valley of Kidron the Mount of Olives is shimmering. They keep going in silence even when they notice that something is happening down there, near the gate. The overheated morning light melts the bodies pouring out of the stone gate into one huge mass; the throng is flowing

can't see what sort of crowd is clambering up the steep road. The fresh air is alive with the song of larks, but the roar propelling the endless crowd toward them can already be heard clearly, as if the earth were rumbling; they are coming closer and closer. The three of them are standing still, waiting. None of them speaks. Children are racing ahead. Naked striplings. Panting up the hill. Simon and his two sons are sucked into the din; a grotesque lunatic is hopping, flitting about, screeching and squawking like a bird; the pounding of feet. Upward rolls the cloud of dust, pulling the crowd into itself. Faster! Let's go! Inside a ring of soldiers three men stripped naked are gasping; the waist cloths have slipped to the side, no longer covering their loins, and sweat draws stripes across their bodies, following the traces of flogging; they're dragging their crosses on their shoulders, blood oozing from the shoulders, bruised flesh flashing bright; the pointed bottoms of the crosses grate, jump on the stones, bump into one another; the clicking and snapping of sandals. I can't! Come on! Screaming, the people shove and push the people at the head of the procession; everybody wants to see everything, and the soldiers are also helpless, maybe they even enjoy a little a confusion and turmoil which for once they don't have to quell. Simon looks at Rufus, and his voice, as always when addressing his son, is instructive. Sinners! he says softly, and repeats, Sinners! The officer in charge—the effects of his morning exercises cancelled out by days of voluptuous indulgence—is tired now, out of breath. He, who's supposed to be running things here, he too is being shoved along by the filthy mob. How do you know, Father? Rufus asks, offended by the paternal tone. How do you know? You were there when they committed their sins? Simon's eyes cloud with fury. The beautiful mouth is sharply insolent and tops off the words with a smile. When the officer glances at Simon their eyes lock, two raging beasts. The officer pumps as much air into his lungs as he can, and Simon is about to cry out when the officer shouts over the noise: Halt! A peaked helmet and a drenched, disgustingly clean-shaven Roman face flash through the clouds of fury darkening Simon's face. With a protective, haughty gesture Simon raises a hand to his chest. As if to say, What have I got to do with you? The officer doesn't know yet what he wants. Simon can smell the unpleasant odor rising from the other's body. Shalom! says the officer, peace be with you, grinning, but Simon does not reciprocate, which is a great insult, for the Roman has learned Aramaic well. The jumble of sounds subsides; the silence of the crowd is heavy and ominous, which surely means that something must happen now. You know who is going by here? Do you know who we have here? asks the officer, and smiles, glad to be able to catch his breath. In case you don't, I'll tell you. Your king! A curtained palanquin

had sent it again. He sent me what he had sent to Simon one thousand nine hundred and eleven years earlier. That's when the Lord linked me up, there, on that horseshit-covered road in Saalfeld, with those two Simons of yore. Because I seized what one of those Simons rejected. I seized what the other Simon seized nineteen hundred and eleven years earlier. That's how the two Simons were united in me. And I knew that death was not my fate, because I had died when I was born, and my death, when I die, will be followed by my life. That's why I'm not looking forward to death, but neither do I fear it. And what could Grandfather possibly have known of all this? What could he have known on that bench under the mulberry tree? What? But let's get back to where we were! We're in, inside the gate already! Come on! Don't look at me! Come, push along with me. We left off with Rufus struggling forward with his sickle, following his father, whom he cannot see. He is shoved and pushed by the people climbing up the hill, and he has to be careful with the sickle. And then he sees the girl whose bodily perfection his hands long to touch, then he sees Rachel—a very beautiful name, Rachel: it means mother sheep, a ewe. Rolling, crunching stones under the running feet. Rachel is running, frightened, looking for somebody, probably someone she's been separated from; but it's Rufus her eyes find. Raising the sickle above his head, pushing with his shoulders and treading on

feet, Rufus makes his way to her. With his free hand
he grabs Rachel's hand, presses this miracle of delicate
little bones, soft flesh, and hot skin, he yanks her and
pulls her along after him until they manage to tear
themselves away from the crowd. At the side of the
road he lets go of the hand that has nearly melted in
their common sweat, but the sickle—so flustered, poor
thing!—he's still holding above his head. The rabble
surges on, is blocked, backs up, then resumes its push
forward, the rear brought up by stragglers trying to
keep up: the blind and the lame. Last of all is a leper
who, as he's supposed to, keeps shouting as he races
forward on his rotting feet: I'm a leper! Leper! And
then the road empties out, turns white in the dazzling
light. Murmuring noise from the top of the hill. Larks
can be heard again, as though their song had never
stopped. And the two of them are just standing there.
Beautiful, isn't it? Isn't it? Of course this is not exactly
the way my grandfather told me the story. He couldn't
have known what I know now. But I've kept thinking
about it and I've come to the conclusion that this is
the only way it could have happened. Accurate memory helped me in this. All my grandfather said was that
in Jerusalem there lived a Simon who had two sons.
One of them, whom they called Rufus because he was
a redhead at birth, took for his wife the beautiful Rachel and went to live in Rome. Because at the time one
of Rachel's uncles lived in Rome. He had a big house,

them money against a letter of credit. And so with no further mishaps the family arrived in Rome. Of course the uncle could not have known that one third of Simon of Cyrene's wealth would be swallowed up by the Pamphylian Sea, and that he would be stuck with some of the debts the newcomers had run up on the way. They were given a small room in the big house, but they were glad because the little room opened into the atrium, like all the others, and in the middle of the atrium a fountain was bubbling quietly. In this house Rachel gave birth to a girl, whom they called Yael, or wild goat that skips about on the hard rocks. The uncle was laughing behind the backs of his poor relatives: the ewe gave birth to a wild goat? Wonder who covered her? Caiaphas grew up to be beautiful, as his father had once been, but his beauty was soft, like his mother's before she had her children. At night he'd seek out the company of Macedonian slaves and hang around the theater; he knew how to imitate and mimic everybody, could sing and dance; in the end he disappeared, and people said he'd become an actor, but unfortunately not just an actor. Yael lived up to her name, too. Nobody knows where or when, but a youth from a prominent family fell in love with her. The young gentleman's name was Caius, a very popular name among Romans. He was proud not of his family but of his name. It was the same as that of Caius Marius, who was elected consul seven times because, allegedly, as a child he had found an eagle's nest with seven cheeping eaglets in it; and Julius Caesar was also Caius, Caius Julius Caesar, who was a relative of the great Marius, and therefore, to some extent, related to me, too; though they did not know each other, Caius was part of another, the next generation; but already in his early youth Caius took Marius as his model, the Marius who, as I've said, is my relative! Our stupid little Caius chose as models the two great ones so that, by holding forth about them, his own insignificance could bask in their greatness. So what we have here is this love, this mutual passion between the slow-witted Caius and quick-witted Yael; Caius is rich, Yael poor; Caius obtuse, Yael intelligent; Yael industrious, Caius lackadaisical. Caius seemed to expect that, because of his famous namesakes, the gods would raise him overnight to the rank of consul or praetor; he knew nothing about handling weapons and he was a lousy orator, but while Yael was tiny and slender, Caius was a giant of a figure, though his face was not so powerful as those of the other two Caiuses whom he carried so hopefully in his heart; however, his obtuseness was coupled with a certain kindliness and his face was girlishly hairless. To a hairy Jewish girl this could be very attractive. Though your name is Caius, the sharp-tongued Yael told him, you're beardless like Clodius, and your passion, like his, rises not at the prospect of power but at the sight

the father still remembered well, and because the baby girl was so beautiful even in the crib that people came to marvel at her, he named her Rachel in memory of the Rachel who was the first to come to Rome and thus, in a way, may be considered a progenitress. This young man had no other children. And to make sure his little girl was not taken from him, he took on the Christian faith, but he could not keep down the flesh of pork. He had to vomit it out. In his distress he sent a letter to Sura asking for the advice of the sages as to what Jews should do in their desperate straits, how they might keep the commands of their faith in the face of persecution. The reply took ten years to arrive. It came not in the form of a letter but in that of a merchant who wasn't really a merchant but a famous Gaon, and his name was Samuel ben Josef. In the meantime, Rachel had grown into a beautiful girl, and of course Samuel, who was given lodging in the house of the letter-writer, immediately fell in love with her. And this is how Samuel spoke to the assembled Jews: Remember! Enoch and his cohorts fell into the sin of idolatry, for which the Lord withdrew into the third heaven. And what do we call idolatry? If men, themselves creatures of the Lord, worship not the Lord but certain of His creatures. Living or dead. It is as if the Lord had fulfilled the promise of the curse and taken you among a people that neither you nor your fathers had known before, and where, as it is written, you will serve strange gods, even trees and stones. And what about dissembling? To dissemble is to lie, and it is also a sin, the Mishnah tells us. Therefore you are committing a double sin, and there is nothing I can do except to reprimand you most severely, and to pray for you. And now, until the sheep return to the fold, I shall stay here. And so he did. Rachel gave him twelve children. But thirty years later Samuel set out again to return to the Academy of Sura, where he had been a famous teacher before he left. They took the little ones with them. His two oldest sons, well-respected rabbis, stayed on in Cordova. But no news ever came from Sura or anywhere else, and the traces of Rachel, Samuel, and the little ones were lost forever. Maybe one day we'll discover them and they'll come back. Whenever someone knocks on your door, don't be surprised, you never can tell. Don't be surprised if in your dreams you speak in unfamiliar languages— Aramaic, Hebrew, Greek, Arabic, Latin, and, because of later times, many other tongues. It may be only a dream, but everything is true and everything is probable. So don't be amazed!"

ering soap on his hair, I can hear the sounds of the soap and I can feel somebody watching me. Can I turn around? The woman with the glasses is watching me, and next to her, on the same chair I was just standing on, Uncle Frigyes is sitting. He's laughing. He jumps up and runs out, vanishes in the dark. I can feel that it's me in there, in the dark, it's me he's hugging, and now he forces the toothbrush into my mouth, breaking a tooth. Maybe I'm bleeding? Uncle Frigyes is laughing. I *am* bleeding, I'll bleed to death, it will all flow out. I am lying down somewhere. The stone is cold. I've no idea how I got here. A whole lot of things are happening, but I can't even move, all I can do is watch. Dark. Somebody is yelling, "If you cut your finger with a knife it would hurt, wouldn't it? Answer me!" "Yes, it would!" How interesting: it was my voice that answered but I can see my face, and the face didn't open its mouth. "That's how I'd cut into you, just as that knife did!" Maybe it was Grandpapa who shouted, "Yes, it will hurt!" Now I know where I am. The biggest pot is on the stove. The frying onion is turning black. So it was just now, after all, that I slid down the railing and fell all the way down here. But I'm waiting in vain, she cannot come, Grandmama is lying in her room, and if my blood keeps flowing like this I will die, too. So, it must have been now that I cut my finger. But this white leg is not of a person. A bed. Seems to be in our kitchen. They brought the beds from there. In the bathroom, too, the floor tiles are black and white. Where the fish still is. But at the windows curtains are billowing in the wind, the sun is shining into the room, the bloodstains are fluttering in the wind. Ten white ones. Double bunks, white walls. Nobody around. With nobody absent there would be twenty boys living here; there's always one of us in the sickroom. Must step only on the black tiles! Must wait. Somebody will come and then I'll leave, too. Strolling among the beds, stepping only on black tiles, never on white ones! But then I must not be here, after all, because this woman hadn't appeared yet, and I don't know why she's here; and if she's leaning over me, then I must be lying down. Lying somewhere. Her mouth is moving. Over black-and-white squares. It feels as if I'm lying right in the middle of something soft and white, but still on the cold stone, and this woman seems to be saying something; I can see her mouth move but I can't hear anything. Grandmama, she's the one who brings the chamber pot because I have to pee. Still, it's Grandpapa who is lying in the bed, not I. But how did the beds get there? Who did this? That's the way he always lay. Doesn't notice the fly landing on his eye. Has to be shooed away! He keeps looking because his eyes can't be shut. Grandmama covers the mirror, too, with a black kerchief. I don't know where the flies are coming from. Grandmama is waving a black kerchief, pulls the shutters to, though I'm sitting here, but it's not him! something is lying there, something that resembles me or *is* me. I should do something! Jump up! But something holds me down. I can't make a move. I'm sitting here, or lying there, because the whole thing could be some mistake, and I failed to notice that in the meantime a son was born to me, and a grandson, and I've grown old and died and now that boy who is me is looking at me. Or maybe I've just gotten sleepy, Grandmama told me to stay here, and I've been dreaming and now I'm waking up? Where could I go? But Grandpapa is sitting in his armchair, his hand on the maroon velvet. But that's not Grandpapa's hand, it's mine! But Grandpapa suddenly snatches his hand away, a cup is tipped over, and in his fury his neck and mouth turn black. "You can't say that! You should have understood by now that I'm myself, me, *me*, ME!" But Uncle Frigyes closes his eyes and wheezes. "I only said it to get your goat, because when you're furious you can feel that you're alive!" Grandpapa is not laughing. "This is serious. Go ahead, laugh! And don't try to hide your laughter, either, it's as sharp as a knife! That's exactly how you tell me—with that suppressed laughter, you knife!—that all my ideas, my whole life has been one big mistake!" A gray shadow scoots behind the beam. The shadows are rejoicing. A whimpering voice: Grandpapa, let's have a story! Grandpapa, I can't remember anything! I can hear it, this whimpering voice inside me, and Grandmama was still not coming and then maybe I was just dreaming, after all. The shape of the body showed very distinctly under the cover, and the clasped hands sank into the softness of the blue silk; weight; flies on the wall and on his forehead and around his nose. The flame of the candle, its tiny crackling noises. Outside, the sounds of the wind, the light filtering in through the slats of the shutters, and the little rumblings of my stomach. I didn't get breakfast. It's something Grandmama forgot today. Once I ate all the whipped cream, while the two of them were fighting, but I threw up that evening. Uncle Frigyes always dropped lots of crumbs on the carpet. He broke the challah into crumbs and gesticulated with a piece in his hand. "Serious, you say? I don't know, my dear, if there is anything in the world we humans can talk about seriously. I prefer to laugh. At you. I'm laughing at you, too! Mistake? You mean an error, deviating from the truth? But what truth? Your whole life a mistake? Your ideas? Ideas can be directed only toward some goal. But who knows what the goals are? Maybe God? You've called it a mistake, my dear, not me. Ideas and mistakes, goals and truth, these are the two couples of the quadrille. Dancing gracefully. If you like your own ideas, then let doubt be yours, too. I have no doubts, because I have no ideas either, and I have no ideas because I see no goals, and since there are no goals, I don't know, I know nothing, so I've entrusted myself to God. Are you familiar with the Portuguese story?" "I am!" "I'm thinking about Simon Maimi, who died, walled up in a dungeon, but did not convert to Christianity though the other Jews did!" "I know the story, that Simon is a distant relative of mine! But how dare you preach to me? And what are you talking about, anyway? Did I set the fire under the stake? I did take off my clothes, but I never shed my faith! That's only a secular pretense! I got as far as my own soul. My own! All the way to my soul that turns only to God! And this soul, private, and my own, cannot be ranked with any herd or flock!" "Be quiet! Let me continue!" "Don't bother, I know the story very well!" "The end, you don't know the end of it!" "The end of what? It has no end!" Grandpapa yelled. Uncle Frigyes was also shouting. And they wouldn't let go, kept pulling and squeezing each other's hands among the cups and utensils on the table. Uncle Frigyes dunked the challah into the coffee, and when it soaked up the coffee he ate it. Grandpapa's denture was in a mug next to the candle. Grandmama said we'd put it away because everything that's left of Grandpapa is a memento. Uncle Frigyes would also roll little balls out of the challah and bombard Grandpapa with them. They were laughing and Grandmama said she wouldn't come and sit with them because she couldn't stand the way they were behaving. Like idiots. "*Ruhe!* You can't possibly know the

rance." Uncle Frigyes was as tall as Grandpapa, but he was fat. When Grandpapa died Uncle Frigyes couldn't come over because he wasn't alive either, but Grandmama said she didn't want to tell me about it before. I don't know what happened to his watch. He probably died while we were eating the fish and the phone rang. On Friday. Fat people had to have special coffins made for them, Grandmama said. On his large belly an additional little bulge. That was the watch in his vest pocket. That watch struck every half hour, playing a little tune. As if his belly were making music. When he came and settled in the armchair, he'd draw me between his legs and I had to put my head to his belly; then he'd detach the watch chain from the button of his vest and hand me the watch. While they talked I lay in bed and waited for the watch to make music. When it struck I closed my eyes and the tune followed in the dark, but my joy was short-lived, for the tune was quickly over and then I had to wait again. We finished the coffee and the two of them were holding each other's hands. It was Grandpapa telling a story now. "I don't know if I've ever told you that on the way home I came through Cracow. In front of a house there was a huge crowd. I stopped, too, to see what they were gaping at. A bomb had created a perfect cross section of that house, so that in the intact halves of the rooms you could see pictures hanging on the wall and pillows scattered on the sofas, all a little dusty; on the third floor, I don't know why, a chamber pot was right in the middle of a table with a singed lace tablecloth; on the fourth floor in a room with silk drapes there stood an upright piano against the wall. In the split staircase a man was going up, that's what the crowd was watching, and I directed my attention to him, too. He was an older man; he stopped at every floor, rested, then moved on. On the fourth floor he put his key in the lock, opened the door, then shut it behind him. In the hallway he hung his coat on the coatrack. Went into the room. Looked around, smiled, drew his finger across a chair, noticed how dusty it was; then he sat down at the piano and opened the lid. He looked at the keyboard for a long time, sunk in thought. Those of us down on the street were standing and watching in complete silence. I think the Poles knew who he was. And then he began to play, I think something by Chopin. But he was playing for himself, practicing, getting his hands used to the instrument. When he missed a note he'd start over again from the beginning, and that allowed the same melody to show its many different sides. This made the whole thing more beautiful. The crowd was growing, really swelling. Many people cried. The strange performance lasted for more than an hour. Then the man got up, stretched his back and pelvis, and started for a door, which opened into air. And he yanked the door with him, frame and all, and the frame yanked with it the

the tub, but the light woke it up. "Grandmama managed to get fish!" "No need to clean them, because I must leave early in the morning!" He gave me his clothes, and there he was standing naked, and I liked to see him naked. Grandpapa said that according to the Torah nobody should see the nakedness of his father. Éva said that nakedness meant the prick. "Could I sleep with you then, Father?" "I almost forgot, I've brought you something. Give me my pants! And run some water in the sink. We'll put the fish there for the meanwhile." While he was looking in his pants pockets for what he'd brought me, I filled the sink with water, but didn't look back, just waited to see what the present might be. It was something like the cartridge Csider once gave me, only empty. "It's a whistle. Blow it!" In the sink, the fish was flopping about, wanting to swim but didn't have enough room. In the shower my father was standing with his eyes closed. I sat on the chair and occasionally blew the whistle so he could see I was glad to have it. I was so excited to be sitting there, because there he was soaping himself and tonight I could sleep in the same bed with him. And then the door opened a crack and I saw Grandmama blinking in the light and shouting, "Feri! Feri! And you, what are you blowing that whistle for in the middle of the night?" But instead of coming in she ran back out. The whistle vanished. At night there was no kerchief or hat on Grandmama's head, and when she

the towel around his waist. Grandmama ran behind him. Grandpapa made a big effort to keep up, too. From here, from the bathroom, I saw the room I'm so rarely allowed to enter. When Grandmama was cleaning it I'd go in with her, or in the afternoon when everybody was napping. The nicest room in the house. There is no carpet, with every step the floor creaks, and the whitewashed walls are completely blank. No curtains at the window, no need for them because the sun doesn't come in here; outside, three enormous pine trees, and the dark shadows of the pines move on the walls inside the room. Here I can be relaxed; nobody can slip behind my back. On the big bed a soft green blanket. Just to be lying there and imagining that he is there next to me. In front of the window a long table on nice bentwood legs, and the cushions of the armchair covered with the same soft green as the bedcover. The tabletop is clean, empty; there is only one drawer, but it's always locked, because that's where the most important papers are kept. That's where I stole the Nina Potapova textbook from, on a Sunday morning. Csider can search in the attic all he wants; everything that's secret is here, but I can't tell anyone that. And there's nothing else in the room. Still, when we light the chandelier the whole place glows, nice and not too brightly. Again Grandpapa said something and stopped in the middle of the room, under the light of the chandelier. Father tore the towel off his waist.

gram. It always came unexpectedly. The small room with all the closets and the sewing things was dark and hot. I was running toward the room that was light, because suddenly I wanted to see his eyes. "How should I talk, dear God? As in prayer, I would like to ask that You put the words into my mouth!" When he let me lie next to him and he hadn't turned the light off, I'd always look at his eyes, because I couldn't understand what made them so blue, what could that be? "Oh, son, please put on your pajamas, you'll catch cold!" Then, that Sunday morning, I snuggled next to him in bed. He was lying there naked. I would have liked to take off my pajamas, too, but was scared to, I don't know why. That way I could have felt him more. I dug my head into his shoulder, I could smell the cover, and I pressed my body on his. But he quickly pushed me away. "Get out of here! Go! Get back to your bed, go on! Get out of here! Go!" He took the pajama pants from Grandmama and tossed the wet towel into the armchair, but it fell on the floor. "Cat got your tongue?" "Again? Are we starting again, Father?" "I'm terribly frightened! I know what's awaiting you!" Father unfolded the neatly ironed pajama pants and, as if trying them for size, covered his lower body with them; he thought for a long time, burst out laughing, then waved the empty pants before Grandpapa. "Come on, Father! I'm sorry, I just can't help laughing. What do you know, reciprocate! what you got in return was that you could happily admire yourself! because with selflessness you don't have even a nodding acquaintance, your every act is hypocrisy and a lie, you've always protected your virginity because you're a coward, always have been! I hate your impossible flowery rhetoric, your filthy desires sublimated into spirituality! You've never lived, haven't you noticed? You have never lived! Yes, you've been around, but you've never lived! If I didn't take into consideration that unfortunately you're my father, then right now, as befits a murderer, I'd slap you good and hard and make sure your shitty thoughts spread no further, not even to *my* ears!" "Hideous! My God, could I be that guilty, am I that guilty? Will I be arrested by my own son? Here, here I am." "Get your hands away! Don't be a martyr! Not for me, not even that! You make me sick! Do you understand? I'll tear you to pieces as I'm tearing up this rag. Get the hell out of my room, you hear?" I was holding on to the door. Grandpapa spread his arms. Father ripped his pajamas in two. A strange thud from the bathroom. The fish was out of the sink, thrashing about on the floor. I was holding the fish, but it was slippery, it wouldn't let me help. I pressed it against me, and put it back into the tub, ran the water for it. Grandmama was crying and ran into the kitchen. My pajamas were slimy. Father slammed and locked all the connecting doors, locking himself in his room. When the tub was filled up, the fish began to swim. It was quiet. This is where Grandpapa told me the story of the fish-smelling girl. It was when Grandmama had gone to the market that up in the attic Grandpapa told me the stories about our ancestors, the day Grandmama brought home the fish. "I'm telling it to you as my grandfather told me in Szernye, on the bench under the mulberry tree." Grandpapa was sitting on the chair I had sat on when Father was soaping himself and the fish was flopping around in the sink. But now he was whispering: "Don't look at me! I don't exist any more!" I was looking at the black-and-white tile floor. The skylight was made of wired glass. I couldn't imagine how they had got the netting into the glass. I kept looking at it. That's where the light was plummeting down, slanted, into the attic. Now! Now! Now it's rushing down! It would be great to see the instant when the light began, or when it ended. "Don't look! Just listen! The story has no end, it will continue in you, and you may pass it on. If you can. Let me go on, then, still as my grandfather told it to me. I almost said to myself, Watch what you're saying! watch your mouth! when you say that the two oldest sons of Samuel ben Josef stayed in Cordova. Is that what I was saying?" "Yes!" "That's how I answered back then, too, but this is how my grandfather from Szernye continued: Then I made a mistake, for while they planned it that way, that's not what hap-

its hide. We'll add to that and buy another one. Judah, who was more sensitive than clever, argued, How can we sell its hide while it's still alive? How? And if I'm crazy, then just go on by yourself! I'm going to a doctor! Reuben burst out laughing. Why would you do that? Who's sick, you or the donkey? By now Judah was shouting, I'm taking the donkey! Reuben continued with his teasing: Yourself? Donkey to the doctor? The doctor's no jackass! Judah took off at a run, tugging and pulling the sick donkey after him and yelling, Go ahead, go on by yourself! I'll manage! I'm not going with you! Reuben got on his donkey and trotted off in the opposite direction, but not before shouting back, You're as dull as your donkey! King of Donkeys! That's how Reuben returned to Cordova. And that's why Judah stayed in Cádiz, because of the sick donkey. A little boy showed him the way. They strolled across town—the boy in front, followed by the donkey, Judah ogling at everything, trudging behind them. They had gone past all the houses when the little boy stopped. There! That one! That's the house! A path led to it, bordered with olive trees and bountiful wildflowers. When the bearded old man standing in front of the house learned that the donkey's owner was the son of Samuel ben Josef, he bowed and said nothing for a long time. I don't know, he said finally, I only hope I have enough knowledge to cure the donkey. I am acquainted with, and greatly

and a weasel running around at their hooves; also a few tuft-tailed polecats and lots of squirrels. And in the fourth room, fish were swimming in a pool: the stingray, this frightening black pancake, and pretty starfish, and carp, sea bream, perch, trout, bullhead, and gudgeon, and squid with a hundred tentacles, and soft jellyfish—a very pleasant company, I must say!—and at poolside a stork couple, wild ducks, herons, and white seagulls. Judah was amazed. As if this were the place he had been looking for all along. As if in my dream, my days were spent in marvels and miracles, truly, and I felt at ease because the donkey got better and gradually regained its strength. And in the fifth room, in the midst of the wild noise and infernal stench of the animals, in front of the window, sat the pale-faced girl. With golden thread she embroidered fine silks with patterns of plants, nothing but plants. And I learned much from the old man, too. I learned that there's poison in the fangs of the cobra, and it can be used to cure leprosy; and the liver of hedgehogs, mixed well with isinglass and pulverized, is an excellent remedy for donkey ailments. And he also taught me that parrot droppings relieve toothaches, and the venomous secretion of flatfish, smeared on a cow's rear end, can ease her calving pains. Disorder? shouted the old man in the animal cacophony, this is God's order! Judah also liked to sit next to the pale-faced girl. The girl looked up: You've asked me, Judah, why I keep at this embroidery day after day. I don't know myself, since those who wear it die, every one of them, and the silk and the gold stitches decay along with their bodies. I think I should embroider the wind, that's what I think, and then everyone could see my patterns, see the many tendrils, buds, and flowers of my soul glowing and fluttering gently about us in the air, against the great blue sky. Yes, that's how beautifully she spoke. Judah asked her to be his wife, and from her he learned all about plants. Later our old father died and the two of us were left there among the animals. And they all lived happily together. In a big book Judah noted down everything he experienced, the things he already knew and even those he hadn't yet learned, all the great life questions that remained. He hardly noticed that in the meantime four daughters were born to him, because the animals were also multiplying in great numbers. As though in passing, the owner of a sick bull told them that Tarik's hordes had crossed the sea and might pose great danger. And one night Cádiz was set on fire. The animals bellowed, moaned, squawked, and screeched. Only the crocodile stayed calm, though lazily it opened an eye. The flames of the burning city illuminated the inside of the house and Judah's daughters wept, even though here, among the animals, they were never afraid of anything. Only the shadows of the animals on the wall, that's what we were so frightened of! The wildcat jumped up on the roof and growled. And then a sooty shadow of a figure stopped by our house and shouted inside, Whether you stay or run away, make sure you keep to yourselves, keep apart! Don't get the rest of the poor Jews into trouble! But why? our father called back, surprised. Wasn't it you who gave the Visigoths' secret battle plans to Tarik? the breathless stranger managed to say before taking off. But our mother was very calm as she went from room to room. First she opened the cage of the turtledoves and pigeons and said, Go on, fly! Then came all the birds of the meadow and forest. She released the monkeys, and the monkeys somersaulted away into the red night. The serpent slid under the door and silently vanished. The antelope ran to the north, the grasshoppers popped off in all directions, the insects crawled about briskly or took to the air if they had wings. Only the crocodile showed some reluctance, but your grandmother kept poking at it until it finally dragged itself outside, looked around, oriented itself, and set out for the Nile delta. When only the ever-silent fish were left, Great-grandmother looked at Great-grandfather. We're ready! And they loaded up the white donkey and the family took to the road. To Uncle Reuben in Cordova. Of course one should know that when it's night in Cádiz, it's already dawn in Baghdad. And who would have known that the tramp Shaprut would decide to leave Baghdad that dawn, his destination unclear even to himself. Shaprut is a young man with all his possessions on his back. Shaprut cannot sleep in the same bed two nights in a row. Always on the road, his eyes burning with an inner fire, his eyelids, irritated by sand and light, always red and bleary. Where are you coming from, Shaprut, and where to now? I don't know. Blindly ahead. Following my nose. I think that's the safest direction! But no matter how many miles Shaprut would cover, the earth is round—of course Shaprut couldn't have known that—and just by walking he could never leave himself behind, and that's why there was no place where he would find what he was looking for. Six years later he wound up in Cordova. There he asked not only for lodging but also for the hand of Judah's oldest daughter. Could this be what he had been looking for? The young couple slept together for two nights in a row, and for two days in a row Shaprut told stories. One day I'll tell you Shaprut's stories. And then he disappeared again. He left not a single trace behind, only a germinating seed. When this seed sprouts, six months from now, we shall be entering the second circle. Because the story has seven circles. My grandfather told me about six, and the seventh is ours. The first, Rufus's, was the circle of beauty, and that had come to an end, and the end was failure: beauty faded away completely in Shaprut's wondrous tales. The second circle, the one coming up now, is the circle of reason, and in this one,

king: I'm not asking for money, land, gold, a castle, or wealth. My only wish is that if I have the good fortune to cure you, you will come with me to Cordova and make amends with the caliph, whom you consider to be your archenemy and who is my benevolent master. Of course the ballooning king agreed. And the miracle did happen. Though it was no miracle. Hasdai crushed the head of a serpent, tapped a small amount of blood from a lemur, and dried it on the bellies of green lizards, then added some pepper and other spices: the mixture was fed to a pigeon. The pigeon laid an egg. The king ate the egg. In two days he lost two hundred kilograms, and on the seventh day his abdomen was back to normal, and once again he twittered to his servants like this: See how beautiful I am? Am I not beautiful? And this silk waist cloth on my loins is so very becoming, is it not? And happily he went off to Cordova and made his peace with the caliph, which he did gladly, because he could put on airs and haughtily parade his self-declared beauty for the rest of his life. That's how Hasdai was both a great doctor and a peacemaker. Out of gratitude, the caliph made him a minister, so Hasdai became very rich as well. Therefore he may also be called wise. In his free time he interested himself in astronomy, poetry, and translation. Dioscorides' work on botany was given to him by the ambassador of Byzantium; first he translated it into Latin, then turned it into beautifully polished Arabic. Because at that time and place the Jews were Arabs. And he was a magnificent correspondent. It was due to his eloquence that the King of Khazar —ruler of an independent state north of the Black Sea—having read Hasdai's convincing arguments, converted to Judaism along with his entire nation. That's how the Khazars became Jews. And still, there was one great sorrow in Hasdai's life. He had no sons. And the oldest of his seven daughters became pregnant. But they couldn't find out—no! no! she wouldn't tell—who had gotten her with child. And she wouldn't tell, even after Hasdai had beaten her several times in succession. It was as if, in beating this miserable little hussy so mercilessly, Hasdai was taking out his anger at his own birth, his whole life; he was hissing while he beat her. And strangely, the girl did not object to the beating. But why would this bright jewel in the Star of David be angry at his own life? one might ask if one did not know Hasdai's heart. Hasdai's life was ruled by his mind. And the mind—Hasdai couldn't have known this, and neither could my grandfather— is not enough for life. Even when he embraced his wife, twice a week according to the Torah's permissive command, even then Hasdai could not entrust himself to his instincts, because his mind, to the rhythm of his instincts, prayed like this: Let it be a boy! let it be a boy! be a boy, my seed! God grant me my wish! The foolish sin of the mind is the will. And the girl whom he so enjoyed beating and who found pleasure in it, his daughter, was now saying this: What I've done, believe me, I didn't do out of lustfulness, no, Father! Even this beating is better than the pleasure I had! I am your daughter, I am yours! Oh, Father, I was urged on by some kind—I don't know what kind, but some high, highest kind—of reason, Father. I know it's hard to countenance; even your sagacity is inadequate for this, Father! Not even you can know the future! And now I'll be leaving! We thought that the girl had disappeared forever. In Malaga she gave birth to her child, who, for reasons we don't know, was given the name Samuel ibn Nagdela. The family thought the girl had killed herself. In his sorrow, Hasdai established an academy for higher learning in Cordova, the one where Moses ben Enoch spread the wisdom of rabbinical studies. But Samuel did come into the world and it was he—see, the girl was not lying!—who sent the family's fame soaring in intellectual and learned circles. His mind, like a crystal, cut through to all knowledge and also illuminated all knowledge. The mother, working as a lowly servant, did not reveal the secret of his birth to Samuel but sent him to study at her father's academy in Cordova. That's where Samuel and Hasdai met, and the old man was enraptured by the boy and loved him greatly; he didn't know it was his grandson. Yet he must have felt it, because it was to this boy he chose to tell his stories. Therefore,

was of no importance, and she did not reveal his identity to Samuel: I needed him only to have you! With the money his dead mother left him, Samuel opened a small store, but at an excellent location! Sometimes, when I look around, I have the feeling that this is actually Samuel's little store, and I am Samuel, and what was to happen to him then could happen to me now. Here I am, sitting among spices and silks—not exactly local goods!—the gate across the street opens, and a servant comes over from the palace of King Habbus. When he returns to the palace, loaded down with goods, this is how he addresses King Habbus: Sire! Just opposite the palace lives a Jew who's at home in all the sciences, his mind is like the sharpest razor, he writes poetry, speaks reads and writes in seven languages. So the king sends for me and tells me to get rid of this wretched little excuse for a store; he's been looking for a capable secretary for a long time. And I go without a word. And my grandfather was laughing so hard he was plucking his beard. I didn't understand why he was laughing. Of course I quickly remember, said my grandfather, still choking with laughter, that it's not King Habbus who lives across the street but Grünfeld! But that's how Samuel's star rose. First he was only a secretary, but then a minister. He founded an academy, and for its library he managed to acquire the tomes of the Talmud from the Academy of Sura, the same volumes his great-grandfather, the famous

night, on December 30 in the year 1066 according to
the Christian calendar, infuriated Moors attacked the
palace. Granada was in flames. Joseph was rushing
down a corridor when they caught up with him, and
silently murdered him as the dry wind fanned the curtains and the flames. His two children were taken
along by people fleeing the palace. And thus, as the
Lord had ordered, with these children begins the circle
of suffering. They were twins, a boy and a girl, and
very ugly. Their bodies were flabby and fat, their faces
like baked apples that have rolled under the oven
and begun to molder. After six years of wandering
they reached Rouen, where a pious blind old Jew
took them in. When did you last look in the mirror,
Sarah'leh? Must be ten years, still in the palace, by
accident. And you, Simon? I saw myself today, accidentally, while fishing in the lake. I look terrible. And
why are you so beautiful? Because you love me, Shi-
meh'leh! And because I love you, too, you don't look
terrible to me, on the contrary! The Almighty must
have ordered things that way, so they wouldn't have
to hide before the blind old man. They lived by beg-
ging, sitting on the steps of temples, and everybody
gave them something because they looked so hideous
that the sight of them struck horror in the hearts of
healthy people. When left to themselves they hugged,
pinched, and scratched each other, wildly and insatia-
bly. As if the two monsters—don't forget these were

your ancestors also!—wanted to melt into one body! The sick bodies were guided by healthy instincts. The boy got the girl with child. It was possible to make love and even to give birth in silence, but the newborn did cry out and the blind old man heard that. The Jews ran to the house of the beggar. The twins were chased out of the house, the newborn stayed. They hadn't even left Rouen when, by the city walls, the abominable mother was released from this life by a terrible fever and the father, husband to his own blood, hanged himself on a tree. Benjamin was the name they gave the newborn, but although they had it circumcised, no one could decide with absolute certainty whether it was a boy or a girl; it was hunchbacked and completely hairless when it grew up. And Benjamin did not know what sex he or she was. When left by itself, Benjamin was capable of embracing itself, and having gratified all its desires, it would kiss its own hands and tell itself joyously: I am superior to them! What there is separately in others I have together in me! In near delirium, Benjamin would daydream like this: What happiness it would be if I could give birth to my own child, one that I conceived all by myself! And if it weren't for the help of God, if God hadn't helped out at such a terrible cost, then with Benjamin, there and then, the whole thing would have ended, and then my great-grandfather couldn't have told the story in Sátoraljaújhely, and my grandfather

ons purchased with our money are being used first of all not to kill the distant Muslims but for the mass destruction of our people. The noble knights are now gathering around Rouen, clamoring for more loans; in giving them money we know that by this act we are signing our own death warrant. We cannot yet know for what sins the Lord is punishing us. I believe, my wise Gershon, rabbi in Worms, it is a dead man who is writing this letter to you. Therefore we ask you to meditate on these things, to pray and to fast! Thus read the letter brought by Benjamin to the Jews of Worms. Among the fourteen children of this Rabbi Gershon was a hunchbacked girl. It seems she had been waiting just for Benjamin. The rabbi promised a handsome dowry. The money interested Benjamin, but he was afraid: if he married, the secret of his sex would be revealed. But the girl was passionate. Even before the nuptials she spared no effort until, overcoming his doubts, the man in Benjamin won out. The newborn was only two days old—later, Benjamin's son said it was May 18—when Crusaders attacked the Jewish quarter. The woman fled with the baby, but Benjamin's mind clouded over with the knowledge that soldiers were coming; he dressed again as a woman. His body was cut into tiny slices, the earth drank his blood, and his flesh was devoured by hungry cats. The hunchbacked mother and the healthy baby, named David, sailed across the ocean. For fifteen years we

hunchbacked Benjamin, in a basket. If we must perish, at least the news of our fate must live on! This brief sentence may serve as the motto of our descendants." I repeated it together with Grandpapa until I had learned it by heart and could say it by myself: "If we must perish, at least the news of our fate must live on! Listen! They wanted to live! To live, no matter what! My grandfather didn't say—he couldn't have known —but I am adding this: as if the disgrace of living could save you from death! And so followed the age of cunning. Feeling and reason degenerate completely, only the sheer will to live remains. Benjamin wandered for two whole years before reaching Erfurt. There his mouth delivered the message, but his hands were empty. The congregation was saddened by the news, and to help this sole survivor they made Benjamin a guard in the cemetery, paying him two years' salary in advance, a pretty nice sum, saying, Maybe you can do something with this money. Benjamin washed bodies, dug graves, got married, saved up. One child was born to him, a huge blond boy who earned the reputation of a rowdy and drank a lot, played dice, and kept a Christian mistress. Around that time the plague was spreading everywhere. Allegedly, it was Jews who contaminated the wells out of vengeance; Benjamin was washing chancrous, bluish, festering Jewish corpses, until the plague got him, too. Before losing consciousness, this is how he spoke to his blond son, whom he loved beyond words: Everything will be exactly as it has been until now! Everything will be repeated exactly as I tell it but in different forms. I know! In a few days Erfurt will burn, just as in the days of our forebears the cities of Cádiz, Granada, and Rouen burned, the way Worms, Norwich, and York burned! But this is where we left off, in York! When we could no longer hold the castle, the Jews collected all the money they had managed to rescue, and piled it into one big heap along with all their other valuables. This is the MONEY OF THE DEAD, they said, for though we're still living, we are as good as dead. And because you are the craftiest one among us, pass this on to the LIVING. And ask them to pray. That's when I fled with the treasure to Erfurt. But I didn't pass it on then, I am giving it to you now. I'm not dishonest, because you are one of the living, too. But I don't have enough time to tell you my whole adventure-filled story. Behind the cemetery is a solitary oak, you know the tree. If you dig a hole, do it at night, three steps north of the tree's trunk and about two feet deep, and you'll find everything, together with what I have saved since then. My dear child, I speak to you from my deathbed: no more wine, no more drinking, don't drink! And with the treasure go to Vienna and look for Henel, who will give you good advice. And now, I will bless you. My father was crying and I was ashamed because my eyes were dry, but I knew it

bativeness. In Buda. Or maybe we should say that cunning put on a combat uniform? The year: 1251 according to the Christian calendar. We don't know exactly what happened, or how. It's a business secret. But within a few years that seem like a few seconds, the Mendels are lords of Buda. They are tall, blond, harsh-faced. They build their own houses and a big synagogue. In all the surrounding streets—construction is going on everywhere—only co-religionists live, money changers, pawnbrokers, and merchants. With borrowed money many Frenchmen, Germans, Italians, and also a few Hungarians build beautiful homes in Buda. And Jacob begat Solomon. Solomon's son was Judah. And Judah begat a son named Joseph. They all lived long lives. One afternoon, when he is already old, Joseph makes the son of his son sit next to him. They are looking out at the river, with its drifting, crunching ice floes, and the grandfather tells the following story: One bright Sunday King Matthias arrived in Buda. At his side his young wife, Beatrix. We received him on horseback, as the other lords did, but in a separate group. Thirty-one splendid Jewish riders in parade formation. Up front, on a white steed, was your father, and he blew a beautiful tune on his trumpet. He was followed by ten young lads on pitch-black stallions, silver belts around their waists, with buckles big enough to be goblets. Long swords in silver scabbards at their sides, the gold hilts studded with precious jewels. Commanding the detachment, I rode behind them in simple gray formal attire; that's how I had planned it: mine should be simple and formal. On my head I wore a velvet-lined peaked hat, a reminder to the king that Jews in other countries had to wear this kind of hat as a sign of humiliation, but my silversmith, who could hold his own against our Rufus, had ornamented the hat with silver, and in a plain gold scabbard I had the most beautiful of all my swords. Behind me my entourage rode in pairs; on their hats ostrich feathers fluttered, they all wore maroon dress uniforms, and under a silk canopy they carried the Laws of Moses. Then came two armed riders, and finally the servants bearing the gifts I would later present to the queen. The dazzling royal pair stopped at the palace parade ground, by the well. Here, while Judah played his trumpet, I handed them two loaves of bread, a beautiful hat with ostrich feathers, two big stags and two deer, tied up, eight peacocks, and a number of expensive decorative kerchiefs, twelve to be exact; then two men presented the chief part of our gift: a basket woven of silver threads and filled with twenty pounds of pure silver. After Judah came Jacob, to whom his grandfather, Joseph, told the story on a winter evening. After Jacob another Jacob; after him Judah—the Jewish prefects. Their rule was inherited by Israel Mendel, then Isaac Mendel, but by Isaac's time the Turks were at Mohács. The news comes in

there's no man on earth who understands that better than I. Because the circle of annihilation is my circle. And yours, too? Or have you stepped into another one? This we cannot tell, not yet. On the second of September Buda was burning and so was the synagogue where the elderly, the women, and the children sought refuge; the walls came tumbling down. Again a moment when it all could have ended. But I can go on! Don't ask why. Now comes the miracle! In the ranks of the Imperials had been someone as valiant as Dan who fell, as a hero, in the great battle. This man's name is Alexander Simon! Does the name sound familiar? Yes! He's the one! A descendant of the very Simon who had stayed in Jerusalem when Rufus left for Rome. And this is where the divided family, which had been going in two different directions, gets united again. Dan, who died, leaves behind a most beautiful daughter whose name is Esther. The girl escapes from the synagogue, her dress on fire, her lovely black hair singed. Embracing her in his strong arms, Alexander puts out the flames of her dress. And it is also Alexander Simon who pays ransom, simply buys from the emperor the one hundred and forty surviving Jews. The defeated army heads for Nicolsburg, but for Alexander and Esther the retreat is a bridal procession. From Nicolsburg, if you must run away, the road leads to Prague. And from Prague, when they have to escape, their children again set foot on Hungarian soil, and their name is Simon once more. Kőszeg is their home, and then Pest for a while, and then follows the period of peacefulness. The sixth circle of the story. After Pest comes Kassa, or Kosice, then Sátoralja-újhely. That's where Abraham Simon, the miracle rabbi, lives, whose company was sought even by the young Lajos Kossuth, because my grandfather gave everybody wise counsel. And it was my grandfather who moved here, to Szernye; by then my father was alive. We've had this house ever since, and it's been getting larger and larger, who knows how big it'll get? and this mulberry tree, too. That's the story of our family. Since the destruction of Jerusalem it has traversed six of the infinite number of circles. How will it do with the seventh? That I don't know. Perhaps after peacefulness will come happiness, at last. And maybe that will be yours, a great gift from God, after so much trouble. In the meantime, our wealth has dwindled, along with our taste for combat. But we have enough not to starve, and we are still alive, and we go on living. I still feel I'm rich: I have not only all those years—which are now yours, too!—but also God, whom I thought I had lost but then found again. And these years, well, here you are, I am giving them to you. But God you'll have to win for yourself, if He so wills it and if you can. That's when my grandfather stopped talking. The moon rose, red, over the mountains. It was as if I were rising. He didn't know it yet.

heard that? women are so humane! She wouldn't do the actual killing. Oh no, because she's such a gentle soul! But she's strong enough to be the instigator, isn't she? It's my hands that have to put out a life while she—what is she doing? She worries about the table-top!" Grandpapa grabbed the fish, but it jumped and slid from his hand. Grandmama covered her eyes. Grandpapa brought down the mallet. "Your hand, watch your hand, Papa!" I could see her peeking from between her fingers. The head cracked, but the fish was still alive, flinging itself about, smearing the tabletop with its slippery goo. "One more shot and it will be all over. Unfortunately, the eyes popped out with the first blow. So the soup won't taste so good. Fish soup is tastier if the eyes are in it." "Should I make soup out of it?" "If it has roe or milk, yes, add the tail and head—but let's not forget to take out its bitter tooth, that flat tooth behind the gills!—and you can make a nice tart little soup from it." "I'll fry the rest." "Or you can bake it with flour and paprika. Today my stool was normal. Well, then, one last time!" Grandpapa raised the mallet and delivered the blow. The fish wasn't sliding around any more, only its tail was twitching a little. "Here before us lies a dead body. A carp, also known as *Cyprinus carpio*, just as the Latin name for man is *Homo sapiens*. Before opening it up, let us take a look at its exterior. It's fishlike. Its form is functional, enabling it to live in its environment. Except I don't know what the first fish that lived in water looked like. Not quite as fish-like as this? Did it adapt gradually? Or when God created lifeless water did He simultaneously create its living mate, the fishlike fish? Mama, if you please, give us a nice sharp pointed knife! The body of the fish, as you can see, is longish. It belongs to the family of vertebrates. It is thinnest along the spine, its belly, with its vital organs, is the most bulging or convex part. These are the gills, the organ of respiration. Its blood, as you can see, is red, like human blood, only it's not warm but cold. Its skin is covered with scales, laid one on top of the other, from below upward, like the tiles of a roof. If we want to take the tiles off a roof, we have to start on top, at the spine. We, on the other hand, will insert the sharp blade here, at the tail, under the tiles, you see, that's the easiest way to get them all off, from below upward. The equivalent for the fish of your arms and legs are fins. With its tail fin and breast fins it propels itself forward, and this collapsible lobe behind this thorn on its back determines the direction it swims in. But how does the fish rise to the surface or sink to the bottom, if it wants to? With the help of its abdominal fins. These, here. You can see that in its exterior everything is functional and well arranged. And who or what arranged it like this? And when? I don't know! And you should also know that contrary to their reputation, fish have excellent hear-

makes dissection a bit harder. But it's the correct way! And the knife is sharp! We move on easily all the way to the head. Now we could actually cut its head off. Put it aside and we'll examine it separately. Too bad, I can see already that it has neither roe nor milk. Forget the fish soup! Put your hand in there! Don't be scared! Fish is one of your most immediate ancestors, like Grandmama's or mine, too, because in our mother's womb, we are fish for a few weeks; it's like the dark sea bottom, can you feel it? The contents of your stomach is very much like that, too. Now take your hand out. We have to be careful how to tear things out: if the gallbladder bursts and its contents spill out, it turns the meat bitter, this, this dark green thing. With the tip of the knife we remove it nicely, and now we can freely poke around in all the rest. This is the liver, the intestines, this is the heart, and this one's the stomach. The kidney leads into the opening of the cloaca; the fish pees at the same place it poops. And now we nicely ask Grandmama not to grumble but to give us a bowl with some water in it. And now let's take a look at the head. This here is the softest spot, like our neck, it's easy to cut it up. Thank you. In the meantime, let the body swim, if it can! Tap the top of the head! Hard, eh? Inside, a hollow, that's where the brain is. Not much, but enough, more or less, for the fish to manage. Smartly we peel off the disks of the gills, you'll see how beautiful what's under it is, this thing, pretty hard. These crimson arches! You couldn't live in water because you wouldn't be able to breathe. And the fish would drown on shore. Let me explain. There is oxygen in the water, in the air, too. The fish takes in water through its mouth, the water rushes through these fine little crimson disks in which blood circulates, the blood sniffs up the oxygen out of the water, and the circulation takes it to the heart. That's the heart! It has two parts, one's called the auricle, the other is the ventricle. The blood is freshened up by the oxygen, and the heart pumps the fresh blood into every part of the fish's body. The fish lives in water like a fish in water, does all sorts of fishy things which tire the blood, and through the veins the tired blood returns to the heart; the heart pumps the bad blood back here, among the little disks, that's when the cover rises! and the used oxygen that's no longer oxygen goes back into the water. Now comes the ugliest little operation. Cutting it up into pieces. If you take this float, also called the air bladder, and put it out in the sun to dry, you can hit it and it'll give you a nice loud pop. Here you are. Go ahead, take it. In the meantime, Grandmama will prepare the fish." I went out into the garden. The sun was shining. The dog was lying in its house, its muzzle sticking out, sleeping. I squatted down and shoved the bladder under its nose; it jerked its head and opened its eyes. It wanted to eat the bladder, snapped at it, but I ran

Grandmama was calling for me. While we were eating the fish, the telephone rang in the hallway. Grandmama ran out to answer it, but we didn't hear who she was talking to. She called to Grandpapa. I kept eating my fish. Grandpapa said to be careful with the bones. Grandmama told me that once, in her house, before her father was trampled to death by the horse when he fell off the carriage, on Friday evening they were eating fish when suddenly they saw that her father's face had turned blue. As if life had gone out of him, he couldn't breathe and just sat there. Everybody was shouting. And then she remembered what somebody had told her, it was Béla Zöld, that when a fishbone gets stuck in somebody's throat they should slap his back and that would make him cough and the bone either comes back up or goes down. She slapped her father's back and the bone came up, and they continued eating. But when they finished, my mother got up and slapped me in the face and shouted, How dare you hit your father? I laughed, because I tried to imagine Grandmama getting slapped in the face. But Grandpapa said, "What are you laughing at? Do you have any idea what you're doing when you laugh? You know what that is?" "No, I don't." "There, you see? Laughing is one of life's greatest mysteries." But I waited in vain, they didn't come back to the table. I wasn't eating the fish any more, it was very quiet in the house. Grandpapa's chair was still where he had

dow. Maybe if I look at it through the new magnifying glass. A fly was caught in the cobweb. It wants to get away and the spider is at the edge of the web. It's the fly buzzing. Its legs are stuck in the web, no use flapping its wings. Grandpapa was sitting in the armchair. I had a magnifying glass, I used it to watch when I killed a spider or a fly. Afternoon. He pressed his palms between his knees and slept. His mouth was open, his dentures on the table. I was listening to his breathing and observed that when I sit with him like that for a long time then the air goes in and out of my mouth at the same slow rate as does his. Grandmama was calling from upstairs: "Papa! Papa! Come right away! Papa!" Grandpapa closed his mouth, looked at me, and made little sucking sounds. "What is it? Is something wrong? My teeth!" Grandmama wouldn't let up, she kept calling. All the doors were open to create a little draft. "Papa! Papa! Come quick! It's Feri talking!" I ran ahead and Grandpapa dropped his cane and I didn't pick it up for him, and he held on to the furniture and doors. "Papa, Papa, quick! He's talking already! He's saying his name now! Papa!" Grandmama was calling at the top of the stairs and on the radio somebody was talking. Grandpapa stopped at the bottom of the stairs, I ran halfway up. "Papa! Papa! Feri's talking on the radio!" Grandmama ran back and turned up the volume so Grandpapa could hear the radio downstairs. "Let me warn you that you

three kilometers from the town of Gyékényes, near the border, was an abandoned building surrounded by an acacia forest, which locals called the Buchel farm. I also reported to Suhajda that if it was necessary I could have the place furnished overnight." "What happened next?" "Although I had long harbored suspicions of the colonel, this matter could not be suspect since he had mentioned the involvement of Comrade Commander of the Political Group who, I thought, certainly at the time, to be above suspicion." "Let me warn you that you were asked simply to answer the question: What happened next? Refrain from comments and stick to the facts." "Yes. The next thing that happened was that the colonel sent me out and told me to wait in the secretary's office. All I can tell you is that in the meantime he spoke to Budapest, on a direct line, and the conversation lasted approximately twenty minutes." "How does the witness know that Suhajda was talking to Budapest, and on a direct line?" "While in the secretary's office, talking to the secretary, I noticed which line signaled 'busy' on the telephone on her desk. And everyone knew on which line one could talk only with Budapest." "All right. Carry on." "Then the colonel called me back into his office and told me that in light of the urgency of the matter, I should arrange for cleaning and furnishing the farm immediately, because in all probability the meeting would take place within twenty-four hours.

Comrade Commander of the Political Group ordered that the furnishings be the simplest possible. He instructed me to take a conference table with a green felt cover from the quartermaster's or, if there wasn't one there, to get a table like that from anywhere, and also some chairs. And I should have the walls whitewashed if they were dirty. I asked if I should see about some decoration, he said, no, there was no need, but there must be a working latrine." "What other instructions were you given?" "I was instructed that immediately after completion of the job, the detachment setting up the house be ordered to their summer quarters, where, in complete isolation, they should be kept busy with disciplinary, bordering on punitive, exercise. The colonel laughed at this and said it was a brilliant idea, because at least that way the men would even forget who their mother was." "I warn the witness to tell the whole truth. According to police records, the colonel laughed at this because it was the witness's idea." "Yes, I beg your pardon. It was my idea, and the colonel approved it." "Go on." "I was instructed that the whole area must be secured within a few hours, but the troops doing the job should not be allowed to see the meeting site and must not know what sort of task they were performing. The colonel put me in charge of the company. Movement within the secured area was possible only with the right password given at designated times. I myself was not allowed inside the security ring. This arrangement, the colonel said, he would supervise personally. And then he said that we should start without delay, which we did. And by the way, I kept him informed, in detail, of every stage of our progress. Except for one matter. As I've already mentioned, Suhajda's activities had seemed questionable to me since about the beginning of the year. In this case my suspicion was aroused by the speed with which this had to be organized. Also, so far as I knew, important discussions between governments were not usually held in such places. Negotiations of this kind are usually arranged more easily, the governments concerned working through their respective foreign representatives in a neutral country. But what made me most suspicious was this: if what Suhajda had told me was indeed to take place, then, given the political tension at the time, he would surely have had that telephone conversation in front of me, so that I could hear it. As a counter-intelligence officer, I was authorized to hear such things; as a matter of fact, Comrade Minister of the Interior had expressly instructed me to follow the commander's activities closely, if I thought it was necessary. For this reason I ordered a soldier from Unit V to hide in the attic of the farm, to take down in shorthand every word he might hear, and to give his notes only to me; in no circumstance was he to leave the place until I personally came to get him. I found this soldier particularly well suited for the job because he was politically mature and an excellent stenographer." "What was the name of this soldier?" "Tamás Kolozsvári." "Spelled with an *i* or a *y* at the end?" "With an *i*, I think." "The court, at its convenience, will cross-examine this Tamás Kolozsvári. Please go on." "The meeting took place on the night of July 15. I myself was not within the security ring, therefore I have direct knowledge only of the following: at about ten-thirty in the evening, a black sedan came from the direction of Gyékényes and stopped on the road leading to the farm, with its headlights off. Somebody opened the door and gave the password to the soldiers standing at both sides of the road. It was a dark night. The farmhouse was lit only with a signal lamp by which the arrivals could orient themselves." "What kind of lamp?" "A kerosene lamp, at one end of the porch." "Do you have any knowledge as to where and how Henry Bundren crossed the border?" "No. I have no knowledge of that. I was only given a report that two men arrived, gave the password, and reached the house." "Now tell us what happened the following day." "The next day Tamás Kolozsvári reported that his notes were rather incomplete because he had had to jot them down in complete darkness, though he had heard everything very clearly. I myself went to get him, after I had the security ring lifted and the company had left for their summer quarters. While still in the car, Kolozsvári told me that the foreigner had spoken in English and used an interpreter. I managed to get Kolozsvári unnoticed into my office, where in a few hours he transcribed and typed up his notes." "How many pages?" "Fifteen. And it was indeed rather incomplete." "Did you read it?" "Yes. I did." "What were its contents?" "Among other things it said that the Yugoslav instructions ought to be carried out as if they had come directly from the CIA. But the most shocking part was the section dealing with how Comrades Rákosi and Gerő were to be assassinated." "Stop. The notes are in the court's possession. Tell us what you did after that." "For a few hours I was completely helpless because I couldn't think of a pretext for going to Budapest. I wouldn't have dreamed of using the telephone, because by then it was clear that even the direct line was at the espionage agency's disposal. But luck came to my aid. I received a telegram from my mother telling me that my eighty-four-year-old father had died during the night, and asking me to come home immediately. Because of the telegram Suhajda let me go to Budapest. In fact, I had the impression that he was decidedly glad I was going. Here I came directly to party headquarters and gave the material to the head of the Administrative Department. I asked him to have reservist Kolozsvári transferred out immediately, since, besides me, he was the only one who knew everything, and through him the conspirators might get wind of their impending exposure. He took action immediately and within half an hour told me that for the sake of absolute security the authorities had arrested Kolozsvári, who had already been on his way to Budapest. After that I went home and awaited further instructions." "Does any member of the people's tribunal have any questions for the witness? The people's prosecutor? The defense? Accused! Have you any observations?" "None." "Please, take the accused prisoners away. The court will continue its work after a short recess." Grandmama left the room. I got up from the steps. Grandpapa let go of the banister he'd been holding on to. Grandmama came down the stairs and I fell in behind her. "Why did he say such a thing? He didn't come home, then! Papa! Why? Why don't you answer me? Why did he say such a thing, when you're alive? Papa!" "Could I have been wrong?" Upstairs you could hear the radio still saying something, then music came on. Grandmama got hold of Grandpapa's hand. "Papa!" "Could I have been wrong?" "Papa, why do you keep saying that? Please say something, I can't stand it any more! Papa!" "Could I have been wrong?" Grandpapa started for their room, and it looked as if he was leading Grandmama. His cane was on the floor in my room. He kicked it and the cane slid all the way to the wall. Grandpapa sat in the armchair. Pressing his two hands between his knees, he was asleep. His mouth was open and he was breathing loudly, as though something was stuck in his throat. I was careful not to listen to his breathing and maybe fall asleep like him. When Grandmama called him because lunch was ready, he woke up and smacked his lips. He took his denture from the windowsill and put it into his mouth. "Yes. I believe so." "What, what do you believe Papa!" "Could I have been wrong?" But he did show up for supper. Supper, too, was eaten in silence; only when he got up and looked at Grandmama did Grandpapa say something: "Tell me, Mama!" "What? My dear, talk to me!" "Could I have been wrong?" "About what? What are you thinking about? Aren't you going to tell me?" "Yes. I think so. Could I have been wrong?" They closed the door and the bed creaked, and Grandmama kept asking Grandpapa, but to no avail. And then the crack under the door went dark, too. The window was open and I kicked off the cover. "Is this a cricket?" "No, son, unfortunately it's already a cicada, a harvest fly." I tried to walk without making the floor creak. I went into that room, turned on the light, and opened the closet door. The smell of lavender in the closet. The lavender was in small white bags on the top shelf and on the bottom. I stopped to listen if Grandmama was coming, because I heard a creaky noise. Quickly I turned off the light and shut the closet door. But it was only the house, creaking all by itself. There was a small box at the very bottom of the closet and I didn't know what was in it. I pulled it out and all the rest of the boxes fell out of the closet. I stopped and listened again, but I was the only one who'd heard the boxes fall. In that box, folded nicely, a green velvet dress. Its top made of silk with tulle. I took off my pajamas and stood there naked. I pulled on the dress; it was very long. I thought of giving it to Éva. I was scared: If Grandmama comes in now I won't have time to put it back, and if she asks what I'm doing here, I'll tell her I forgot to brush my teeth. On the shelf in the bathroom we had a pair of scissors. With it I cut the gray disks out of the dress. I showed them to Éva and Gábor and lied that they were made of gold and our ancestors had left them here for us, only they painted them gray so nobody would know what they are. Gábor didn't believe it. He tapped one of them against his teeth and said it was lead and could be melted down. Whoever could roll the disk from the door all the way under the sofa was the winner. The door opened and their mother, all naked, walked across the room. In the next room she turned on the radio and we could hear that same voice as before. She put on the same silk robe Éva usually fooled around in whenever their mother was out for one of her appearances. She looked at herself in the mirror and listened to what was being said on the radio. Gábor accidentally slashed the armchair with the sword. She came back, wearing the robe, and sat down in the same chair. She watched the disks rolling. When I went home, Grandpapa was sitting in his armchair. He held out his hand, I went over to him and he hugged me. I could see his eyes from very close. "Could I have been wrong? Dead myths are the most lasting ones! Do you think so, too? Yes. Could I have been wrong?" And in his winter coat he was standing in the middle of the room. But I knew that this room was unfamiliar to me. Somebody was shouting. "If you cut your finger with a knife, it will hurt, won't it? That's how I cut into you, like a knife!" I jumped up and ran toward him, but he was receding. "It will hurt!" Suddenly he was here, very close. His eyes. I put my arms around his neck, and thought my crying would make him feel good. But when I pressed my face to his I felt its stubbles, because he shaved only every other day; he'd just gotten home and Grandmama hadn't cleaned his clothes yet. And I sat up again and realized I'd dreamed this whole thing. This is my bed. Or maybe this is a dream, too. This is my room, with the dark shadows of the trees in front of the window, and my father is not standing in the middle of the room. Something is strange. Grandpapa's breathing. But not strange in the usual way. The crack under the door is dark. Why is he breathing so loudly? As if something is stuck in his throat, wanting to come out but can't. It's just gurgling there, really loud. I listened in front of the door. I could see, in the dark, a body moving under the covers. "Grandpapa!" No

spots. In the bathroom I wet a towel, thinking that this was what a compress was and if I put it on his head he'd be saved. But the telephone didn't work. Grandmama yanked a dress from the closet. With the towel she wiped the thing off his mouth, and now Grandpapa's mouth was shut and the compress seemed to have calmed him down, because he lay motionless. "Don't leave him for a second! The medicine!" Grandmama ran back in. She tried to force the heart drops into Grandpapa's mouth, but they dripped down at the side of his lips. "Don't leave him alone for a second!" I would have liked to hold his hand, but didn't dare. Fingers open, his hands were resting at his side and the pillow was wet around his head, and his forehead and hair were also wet. The gate slammed. Grandpapa opened his eyes again, as if he was listening, and his mouth opened, too, as if he was about to speak. And then he stayed that way. I ran to my room, to the window, to see when Grandmama was coming back. She must be running by the big cross, but it's hard for her because it's steep there. But the gate slammed again. She probably stopped by the cross and turned back because she forgot something. Grandmama covered the mirror with a black kerchief. His eyes couldn't be closed any more, and his chin dropped, though she tied it up. When it started to get light outside, she closed the shutters so it would stay dark inside. A candle was burning at Grandpapa's

then, too, I don't know why. In the evening, when we went to bed, he went past my room on the way to Grandmama. I wanted to hear them, but they spoke very quietly. I ran back to bed when he was on his way out. "You want me to tell you a story?" "No! I don't want you to." He sat down at the edge of my bed and pulled my head into his lap. Then I would have liked him to tell me a story, but it was also good just being there like that, in the silence; strange how he didn't breathe like Grandpapa even though he was his son. "Grandpapa told me stories of all our ancestors, but about his father—who's your grandfather, right? like Grandpapa with me, right?—about him he never said anything." "My grandfather? You want me to tell you about him? All right. Let's see, what shall I tell you about him? Let's start with this. They had an apartment in Hold Street, the whole second floor, a very large apartment. I was afraid of him. He was a small man with a beard and mustache. We also had a great-uncle who was his brother and lived with them because he was a bachelor, never married. Uncle Ernő. I loved Uncle Ernő more than my grandfather. Meals were always around a big table. Father sat at one end of it, Uncle Ernő at the other. During lunch they were always shouting; they were continuing some old political debate, because a long time ago, before I was born, they had spent their mornings in Parliament, on opposite sides, because one of them, my grandfather,

to find his face clean-shaven, and he smelled like the rest of us. But when I opened my eyes I didn't know whether I had dreamed that or not. I went out into the garden. It had rained during the night. Lots of peaches were lying on the ground under the tree. Grandmama stayed in bed all day. Lying down she wouldn't be dizzy and her head wouldn't ache. She put the candy under her pillow, but she wouldn't always give me any. When I said I was hungry, she'd spread some fat or mustard on a slice of bread. I went out to eat in the garden. At night, if I woke up, I'd see her standing by the window. In the evening, after Grandpapa's death, she turned off the lights because she didn't like to waste electricity. She sat down on my bed. I asked her to keep her promise and tell me the story of Genaéva. "On the cover of this book, the book was my father's, was a big angel about to fly up to heaven, and this angel was Genaéva, and when husking corn or just sitting around with nothing to do in winter, my father liked me to read this legend out loud. It began like this: Once upon a time there lived a fabulously beautiful girl, no one had ever seen such a beauty before, ever; her golden hair reached down to her waist, and when she ran, the wind would catch the golden hair and make it fly all around her, but the girl was poor and her parents old. And the old parents died and poor Genaéva was left all alone. One day a young prince rode by. Genaéva happened to be in the

choice but to marry the elegant countess with refined manners whom his father had chosen for him. And that's just what happened, and Genaéva gave birth to her son in the dungeon. One night, while the guard was snoring, Genaéva escaped. She hid in the forest, living on crab apples, wild cherries, and raw mushrooms, and then found shelter in a cave. That's how the two of them lived as the little boy was growing up. Genaéva's long hair was their cover, and soft green moss their bed. But one day Genaéva fell ill. She was so sick she couldn't move. Then a huge rain came from the skies. To get out of the rain, a family of deer sought refuge in the cave, and the hind, the mother deer, heard a little child crying. She suckled him. From then on, they all lived together as one big family, Genaéva, the deer, and the little boy. Until one day the peace of the forest was disturbed by the noise of humans and of other animals. Dogs came barking and yelping, horses were snorting. The deer fled. The good-hearted hind was brought low in front of the cave by the prince's weapon. The hind wept and the sound brought a little boy toddling out of the cave; he was crying, too. The hunting party couldn't have been more amazed. The prince jumped off his horse and went into the cave, where he found Genaéva, whose soul was just being released from the earth by angels. And the prince cried and cried, but in vain. Genaéva's soul was rising heavenward and had time only to say,

Raise him! That child is your son! These were her last words. Whenever I read this story in our house, everybody cried. We got the book from the priest. Yes, my father cried, too. And now I'll tell you my secret. Are you asleep?"

to the pillow. I couldn't move. And it seeped in, under my eyelids. I sat up quickly, which pushed the soft black thing back. This is my bed. This is my room. Again it is waiting—about my head, behind my back —but if I don't close my eyes it can't come closer. Outside, the moon was shining and pressed the dark shadows of the trees into the room. I got up to see whether it was in the garden. White dahlias in the shadows of the trees. As if the white dahlias were telling me where it was. White showing in the darkness. The door was open. Grandmama wasn't standing by the window of her room. Grandpapa's bed was empty. I couldn't see Grandmama's bed from here because that part of the room was very dark. Carefully I started for her bed to see if she was asleep. The floor creaked a little. "Is that you?" Grandmama asked from the darkness. "Yes." "Don't turn on the light!" Grandmama said softly from the darkness. She seemed to speak from a place farther away than her bed. "Aren't you feeling well? Grandmama, aren't you feeling well, Grandmama?" Her face on the pillow turned toward me softly. "A little. Just a little." Her hand moved on the cover, but did not reach toward me. I bent over her, to see her. "Go back to bed, child. Go to sleep." On the night table I groped for the light switch and my hand knocked against a glass, and I thought Grandpapa's teeth were in the glass. "No! Don't turn it on! I don't want you to see it. It's ugly."

as Grandmama had tried with Grandpapa; I was holding them down with my finger, to make them stay, like Grandpapa's; the lamp shone behind the teeth and I could tell she wasn't empty inside, as Grandpapa had been. The kerchief was there, on the chair, the kerchief Grandmama wears at home, but when she goes out she sometimes puts on a hat, too, because she's almost completely bald. Her skin feels warm in my hand. Her teeth still stuck out a little, with my finger I adjusted her mouth, too; maybe that's what she meant when she said, It's ugly. I turned off the light. In the dark I sat in Grandpapa's armchair. After I sat there a long time the room grew light because the moon was shining outside, and I could see Grandmama lying motionless, my eyes got used to the dark. I would have liked to cry, but I didn't let myself because I was waiting for something that might still happen, though I didn't know what. And then I remembered that Grandmama had once told me that a white wall serpent lived in every house and it comes out of the wall wherever somebody dies. I knew it was only a tale, but I pulled up my feet just in case it was true. When I woke up I thought it was a dream, but I was sitting in the armchair and outside it was getting light, and the birds! and I was cold in the armchair, and Grandmama was lying there with the kerchief on her face, the one I'd tied up on top of her head while there was still time. I listened to her and it seemed that all the

found a candle and a sausage wrapped in paper. Grandmama always hid the sausage. I lit the candle at Grandmama's head, closed the shutters, but I couldn't reach the mirror over the commode, and the kerchief slid down. The water was steaming in the kitchen. First I cut off only a small piece of sausage, but I ate it quickly and cut another piece. When I wanted to cut another piece, the knife slipped into my finger. I could see inside my flesh. But the blood bubbled out and trickled across my hand and dripped onto the plate, too. I held my finger high, got off the chair to go into the bathroom. But I didn't fall, only my head was getting closer to the stone, and the door opened, and the floor tiles tumbled down. Black-and-white. Just like the tiles in the kitchen. Gray, sinking into something very soft. The screaming can't be heard any more. It's all nice and cold. They seemed to be taking me somewhere, everything is fluttering and everything I'm wearing is white, but where am I? Somewhere. A car stopped by our gate, but nobody got out and the engine kept running. The garbage man didn't show up the next day. I wanted to dig a hole, but it was raining. Three men got out of the car. That's where I buried the dog, too. One of them stayed at the gate. Two men came along the path between the roses. Maybe they won't take me away. They wanted to ring the bell, but I opened the door before they could. "Anybody else home besides you, kid?" "Grandmama! My grand-

only one person. But not him. I got up carefully; the floor didn't creak until the hallway. The bell rang, but I didn't make a move. If the bell rings it's not him, because he always knocks. If I just stand here, without moving, whoever it is will go away, because they'll think they've already taken me away somewhere, and then secretly I'd stay. And then Father would come. The bell rang again, and the house really didn't like the ringing. I thought I couldn't hold out any more. But I couldn't get myself to open the door, either. In the mirror I could see my shadow, as if I were standing behind myself. "Father?" I asked very softly so only he could hear, if it was him. And though he rang again, I did think it was him. "Father, is that you?" "Open up, kid! I've come for you! Come on! Open up, don't be afraid!" The man told me to get dressed quickly because we're going to Mikosdpuszta and he has to get back. While I was getting dressed he turned on all the lights, I kept an eye on him so he wouldn't steal anything. "Is there an upstairs floor?" "Yes." "Rooms up there, too?" "Yes." "How many?" "Two." I put on my old sandals even though the new ones had rubber soles and the old ones pinched my foot. And he said I didn't have to take anything with me, because I'd have everything I needed there. But I still wanted to take something. While he was turning off the lights I slipped a pebble into my pocket. I had found this pebble in the garden when I wanted to dig

on top of a hill, a big lake under it, and a stream flowing into the lake. The car rumbled over a bridge, we stopped in front of an iron gate. Two children opened the iron gate and we drove up a curving road to the front of the castle. The pebble road was popping under the big car. I could see the lake from here. Another man was standing in front of the castle and he opened the car door for me. A whistle on a red braid hung from his neck. "I'm turning right around," said the man who'd brought me. "Don't you want breakfast?" "No. I've got to get back by noon. Thank you." This other man got hold of my neck. Then the car disappeared in the forest. We were going upstairs on wide steps. He was holding me by my neck. We walked through a corridor, he opened a door and said I should wait in there, they'd be coming for me. He closed the door. I heard the sound of his footsteps, but he didn't go back where we'd come from but continued on in the other direction. This was a big room. The sun was shining in the windows, which had white curtains. Double bunks in the room. Black-and-white square tiles on the floor, just like our kitchen and bathroom. I stood by the door and was afraid to move, though I would have liked to look out the window. It was quiet, as if the whole place were empty. Five beds on one side, by the window, and five on the other side. White iron beds. Opposite the door a table, two chairs; white cloth on the table, a pitcher with water

boy. Didn't say anything, just looked at me. And he lowered his head. The sun was shining brightly just then. His wavy blond hair fell on his forehead and sparkled. He held the doorknob. Then he pulled the door shut. He spoke in a whisper: "You are Péter Simon?" When he asked this, he lazily threw back his head and his hair flew off his forehead and he looked at me again; even like that his hair sparkled above his forehead. "Yes." His forehead was high and curved and smooth, and I would have liked him to come over to me right then. He kept standing by the door. He whispered again: "Come on." I started toward him. The squares were moving under my feet, every which way, black ones and white ones, and that was good, though it bothered me a little that I wasn't stepping on the black and white squares according to the rule; I don't know why, I also felt that I was a little afraid of him. "Well! Come on, then!" He again lowered his head and his hair fell across his forehead. I was standing right in front of him. I could already smell him. Gray spots on his sneakers: mud. But I wanted to see his eyes. And then he pressed me to himself. His naked arms clasped my back. And I hugged him, too, and we just stood there like that. On his chest the undershirt was sweaty, almost wet, but it felt good, and I didn't want to move from there. My arms on his waist; the hard collision of bones and the warmth of his lap, and my face felt the arches of his ribs under the sweaty

body else; any other violation of the rules also had to be reported this way. When we marched into the dining room I didn't know where I was supposed to sit. Long tables and benches. It was hard to climb behind the benches. Cocoa in polka-dotted mugs, then I didn't know that was to be breakfast every morning, and it was so hot we had to drink it slowly. But there was one empty place, that's where I sat. That was also the table where he sat, the dark-faced boy, whose name was János Angyal. When the two days of silence were over, after lights-out he called me down to his bunk, because he was sleeping under me, and said he was born in France, that's why he was here, and he would tell me all about it, but now he wanted me to tell him something. But I couldn't think of anything. Because I felt it wouldn't be a good idea to ask again about that other boy. One had to be careful not to be informed on in one of the boxes; those who had complaints written against them had to report to Comrade Dezső. A whistle hung from Comrade Dezső's neck. When the whistle was heard everybody ran to stand by their beds and Comrade Dezső came with the two big boys who committed the crime against him and the lockers were thoroughly searched. I got clothes, and sneakers, blue ones, another pair of shoes, a toothbrush, soap, and a towel. In the dining room on a huge tray a pile of buttered bread. When Comrade Dezső blew the whistle we could sit down and everyone would try to get the bigger slices, everyone was allowed to have two. The big slices could be folded in two and put inside your shirt, and in the evening, after lights-out, friends could share them. Angyal even had some salt. After lights-out friends would go over to one another's beds. But when there was an alert they would catch this, and also find the buttered bread in lockers or under the mattresses. Anybody caught with buttered bread would get no cocoa the next morning. In the morning we ran naked to physical training. Everybody was embarrassed because that's when the women were coming to work in the kitchen. After the exercise we went running and never knew if we'd go bathing in the lake or not. When we were allowed to, Comrade Dezső would yell: "To the lake! On the run! Not yet, that was no signal! On the run! What is it with you? That was no signal, I said! On the run! Now!" When he blew the whistle we ran. When he blew it again we had to come out of the water. They were watching us very closely because the last one out couldn't go to the lake the next day. That's why all we did was splash one another at the edge of the lake. In the morning, at the lake, all the groups were together. Vilmos Merényi always swam in the lake, alone. Comrade Dezső laughed because somebody always had to be last. But he didn't count Merényi. Merényi climbed out by the bridge and ran back to us from there. I noticed that on one of his thighs he had a thick vein with lots of little branches. Friday, after house cleaning, we went to shower. But starting with Saturday morning we were not to talk or make any sound until Monday morning. We took soap and towels to the bathroom. Angyal said the big boys were doing something in the showers, but I didn't understand what. Once, I said my stomach hurt; when it was the big boys' turn to go, I told Comrade Dezső that my stomach didn't hurt any more, and he let me go with the big boys. The big boys could stand under the showers longest, until all the hot water was used up, because they were the last to shower. But they didn't do anything, Angyal had lied, they only looked at one another. By then Vilmos had gone. One day something happened. We marched down to the dining room and the teachers left. First there was only quiet. The teachers didn't come back. Then the big boys began to horse around under the piano. Only the big ones. Vilmos was also there, and I was watching him. When he crawled out he saw I was watching him and he waved to me. Angyal was my friend, but I didn't tell him I would have liked Vilmos Merényi for my best friend more. I was afraid Angyal might notice this waving. Whenever friends had a fight they would inform on each other in one of the boxes. That day the principal also came into the dining room. We never saw her, even the corridor leading to her office you could enter only with special permission. When I came out through the brown door he wasn't there any more, and all the time I'd been in the office all I thought about was how he was waiting for me. The principal's hair was as if she had never combed it. She was sitting in a white smock, and here too the curtains were white. Her glasses slipped down, she pushed them back; she signaled that I should come closer. I felt the thick carpet under my feet, like the one in Grandpapa's room, and it would have been nice to see if it had the same patterns. "Sit down, my son, let's have a little chat." The chair felt cool. The sun shone through the white curtains and I couldn't see her face too well, or her eyes behind the glasses. I felt as if I were in the middle of some huge whiteness and out of the light a voice was coming toward me. "First of all I'd like to welcome you on my behalf and on behalf of the entire collective of this institution." It was as if she wasn't moving her mouth while she talked. She was whispering. "You must be tired, you probably didn't get any sleep, poor thing. But you'll get plenty of rest. In a few days everything will be all right. I hope you'll like it here. Our strength will make you strong. Here you'll become a hardy and resolute individual. Are you sleepy? Maybe we should talk tomorrow?" "No." "Well, all right, then. In a word, your new life will begin here. To become a useful member of the collective, as if you were born just now, your new life will have to cover over your old life, so that you can be-

now you have to go!" Not in front of the door, not in the corridor, not anywhere. The boy wasn't waiting for me. In the courtyard I didn't find my place for a long time. It wasn't nice to hear the crunching pebbles in the big silence. And then I was standing there, too, with the rest of them. The sun was shining. The boy next to me flexed his knees and then straightened them again. He kept doing that. I stood straight, but later felt I had to do it, too, because I was getting tired and couldn't stand still all the time. The one in front of me was doing the same thing. But from somewhere above us we heard a whistle. "We are not moving, are we?" somebody yelled from above. But the boy in front of me still bent his knees once in a while, and so did the boy next to me. From where I stood I couldn't see the blond boy. The old sandals pinched my feet. The new ones with the rubber soles were in my locker. Somebody must have gone back to the house, because the tomorrow of then was already today. We ran around the courtyard. I didn't know where I was supposed to sit. The boy next to me hid a slice of buttered bread under his shirt. When nobody was looking some boys hissed. Somebody put a hand on my neck. The man who took me to the room. We were walking along a different corridor, down steps. He opened the door to another room. It was dark there. He turned on the light and gave me a pair of sneakers, blue ones, a pair of regular shoes, undershirt, underpants, sweatsuit, soap, toothbrush, and a towel. He wrote things in a book. He held on to my neck and we went upstairs. We walked into a room. I felt it wasn't the same room I'd been in before, but it was very much like that one. He opened the locker, one with five holes, and showed me where I should put everything. But he didn't say anything. Then he put his hand on the upper bunk and gave it a slap. He got hold of my neck again and we were on our way. We crossed the same courtyard and walked into a church. But inside it wasn't like our church. I didn't see any decorations, and in place of the altar, on a long platform, was a table covered with a red tablecloth. Everybody was already waiting, and my place was left empty. And then I was standing there with them. If I tilted my head just a little, I could make out underneath the white paint small patches of colored pictures, like stains. And high up, in the narrow windows, the light was coming through the stained glass. I thought of the window in our attic. We heard the door being shut, but nobody moved, only some of the boys locked and unlocked their knees; me too. From here I could see his hair, but I wasn't sure it was him. I thought of rolling around in the grass with my dog. The iron gate was opened. And we were running, our feet rumbling on the bridge, and the swans swam out on the lake. In a clearing we sat down and the man who had held my neck sat in the middle, and everybody could look wherever he wanted to. Only

teachers sat down, but the principal remained standing and put her glasses back on. She raised her head. I wanted to look at the lamps, to see if they were giving enough light. "We have been silent for two days. The words, the human voice now probably sounds strange, surprising, to all of us." She stretched her hand toward us and her glasses glittered and this made her look as if she was angry with us, though she was talking very softly. "The reason we ordered the period of silence was precisely for this, that what is about to happen now should be memorable for everyone. Please bring up the two pupils from the cellar." Two teachers got up from the table and left, walking quickly between the ranks. While we were waiting, the principal took off and put back her glasses several times and remained standing. The man was coughing. And then they were coming in again from behind our backs, forward. I was afraid it might be him! that he'd been in the cellar! but it was two other boys, their hands tied with rope behind their backs. They went up on the platform and made the two boys turn to face us; both boys spread their legs a little, I don't know why. One of them raised his head high, but closed his eyes. The other one, as if looking for somebody among the rows, kept moving his eyes without settling anywhere. The teachers fidgeted, making their chairs creak. The principal stretched her arm in front of the two boys, but waited for complete silence, for the chairs to stop

facts—before you hear the final decision of the teaching staff. Now then! Friday morning Merényi came to me and told me that Suhajda and Stark had asked him to steal a big knife from the kitchen. Which he did. Is that correct, Merényi?" "Yes." "Their intention was, since they knew that I never lock my door and that from the monitor's table one can see when I return to my room, at the appropriate time, that is to say, Friday night, to charge into my room and kill me with the knife. I told Merényi Friday morning, Go ahead! And Merényi agreed to help set the trap. And this is how it happened! On Friday, Stark was the monitor on duty. He was sitting opposite my room, hiding the knife in the drawer of the monitor's table. Suhajda stole out into the garden, watching to see when I turned off my light. I turned off my light at 9:25. As agreed, they waited another half hour. Merényi, who was standing guard by the main staircase, gave the signal that the coast was clear. Is that how it was? Suhajda!" "Yes." "So then, at ten o'clock Suhajda checked the window one more time and came up from the garden, Stark took the knife out of the drawer and turned off the lights in the corridor. Stark!" "Yes." "Merényi gave another all-clear signal. Then these two approached my room, silently, Suhajda suddenly tore open the door, and in one leap Stark was at my bedside! and stuck the knife into me. He would have, that is, if I hadn't been sitting in the armchair. In that very

room and the teachers had gone off somewhere and the big boys were horsing around under the piano, Merényi crawled out from under the piano and waved to me. And then the principal came downstairs, too. She said the institution would be dissolved because it had accomplished its mission, and everybody would be sent to some other place. But nothing happened. Once in a while a new child would arrive. In the morning we didn't have to run out naked any more, morning exercises were held in the chapel, because it started to snow. Comrade Dezső promised we'd get sleds and skis and then we'd go on a big excursion. One day, after lights-out, Merényi stuck his head in and waved to me to come out. Angyal also saw this. I went out to the corridor, I was already in my pajamas, Merényi was still dressed. He said his train was leaving that evening, he was going to the Rákóczi, the military academy, and if they let him out he would come to see me, and that I should go to the Rákóczi, too. I was afraid he'd hug me again, but we only shook hands, and then he walked away in the corridor. When I got back, Angyal didn't ask what Merényi had wanted. It occurred to me that he might inform on me, but he didn't; that's why he stayed my friend. But one morning after reveille, Comrade Dezső came in and said that as of today Hőgyész and Angyal would change places. So Hőgyész got the lower bunk and Angyal got

screaming. Sat up in his bunk and just kept screaming. Everybody woke up. I'd been just dreaming that a kitten had fallen into the sewage canal and the rest of the kittens, running after it, all fell in; the canal was very deep and the mother cat wanted to go after them, but the ladder going down was made of steel, nothing to hold on to with her claws, and she fell into the dirty water, too. It was still dark outside, very early in the morning. Kolozsvári was sitting up in his bunk screaming and screaming. And then everybody was screaming. They were all jumping up and down on top of the beds and somebody started to throw pillows all over the place. It wasn't me. And all the while everybody was screaming as hard as they could. Pillows were flying. And then I saw that Angyal was on his knees on his bunk and screamed and took aim with his pillow and screamed; he got me right in the face. And I was glad he was still my friend and still loved me. I screamed, too. Picked up the pillow and yelled and jumped up on my bed, and the bed sent me up and up, it had good springs, and I was screaming all the time, and took aim and with all my might threw the pillow back at him. Smack into his mug! The pillow was flying, my foot got caught on something hard, Angyal ducked and the pillow flew right out the window, ouuuuut! the stone floor is hurtling into me, black, white. Scintillation all about me. Then darkness. And the screaming is approaching, receding. Somewhere the door opened, and gray as if in something very soft in this white one right in the middle. Nice and cold. Cracking. Empty snail shell. "Can you hear me over here!" Soft roots, dark, can't go any deeper, can't see out any more. Can not.